DARK WALKER
闇を歩く者

Even though he wanted to turn off the lights, no matter how much he squirmed, he couldn't resist the fingers that moved beneath him.

Written By
HIKARU YURA
Birthday: April 5th
Zodiac Sign: Aries
Blood Type: A
Born and raised in Shizuoka Prefecture

I love dozing off in bed. My favorite luxury is sleeping for hours after a deadline and then getting a massage. My dream is to someday go on a leisurely vacation to a southern island. I hope that day comes soon...

DARK WALKER

闇を歩く者

Written by
HIKARU YURA

Illustrations by
HIROTAKA KISARAGI

English translation by
Christina Chesterfield

June

Los Angeles

DARK WALKER

Written by Hikaru Yura
Illustrated by Hirotaka Kisaragi
English translation by Christina Chesterfield

English Edition Published by:
DIGITAL MANGA PUBLISHING
A division of DIGITAL MANGA, Inc.
1487 W 178th Street, Suite 300
Gardena, CA 90248
USA
www.dmpbooks.com
www.junemanga.com

Library of Congress Cataloging-in-Publication Data Available Upon Request

First Edition: November 2008
ISBN-13: 978-1-56970-615-2
10 9 8 7 6 5 4 3 2 1

Printed in Canada

DARK WALKER

闇を歩く者

Other novels published by
JUNÉ

Only The Ring Finger Knows vol.1
The Lonely Ring Finger

Don't Worry Mama

The Man Who Doesn't
Take Off His Clothes vol.1-2

Cold Sleep

Little Darling

Ai No Kusabi – The Space Between
Vol.1- Stranger

Sweet Admiration

Better Than A Dream

S vol. 1-3

Contents

Dark Walker

The dreams I have when I'm sleeping aren't real. No matter what happens in my dreams, it's not real. And when I wake up...all that's waiting for me is the start of another ordinary day.

He was in a flower garden illuminated by soft light. The faint scent of flowers drifted in the air, and, even though there was no wind, flower petals would sometimes flutter down from the sky. Tomoki Naruse sat in that peaceful landscape, hugging his knees absentmindedly. He was still wearing his pajamas. His body was slender as a young boy's and he had soft, chestnut-colored hair. Long eyelashes framed his big brown eyes, which were a shimmering amber color in the light. A flower petal touched his pink lips, and then disappeared like a fleeing illusion.

Where am I? I don't know why I'm here.

The flowers that spread out upon the ground were as soft as a cushion, and when the white petals touched his skin they felt as smooth as silk. Tomoki softly lay down on his luxurious bed of flowers. He opened his eyes and saw that the sky above him was pearl grey with flower petals flying down as if they were being born from the glittering sky. It was a mysterious scene, like a dream...

XXX will be here soon...

He knew that he was waiting for someone, but couldn't think of their name. *If XXX doesn't come soon, I'm gonna fall asleep...* The air he breathed in was sweet, making him drowsy.

He's always hurt, so I should give him a hug, he thought vaguely, and tried to fight off his sleepiness. No matter how hard he tried, he couldn't remember who "he" was. His eyelids grew so heavy that he couldn't help but close his eyes, and then suddenly he felt a warm hand on his cheek.

"Tomoki..."

He heard "his" familiar voice. He smiled happily, yet still couldn't open his eyes. Tomoki felt a heaviness on his body and "his" breath against his ear. The sensation of the pajamas he had just been wearing disappeared, replaced by the feeling of naked skin against skin. "His" smooth skin felt so good. Tomoki sighed softly. A warm tongue slid into his mouth, making the hairs on the back of his neck stand up. The kisses, the searching fingertips traveling downward—he knew them so well. And he also knew what was about to happen next.

"You're so cute," "he" whispered softly, and Tomoki's lips trembled. "His" fingers and tongue teased Tomoki, and he quickly became hard. He lifted his hips up naturally, as if begging for "his" hard rod which pushed against his abdomen. Since he couldn't see anything, his body was even more sensitive.

"Ohhh..."

"His" hardness entered Tomoki roughly, and Tomoki let out several small gasps, as if trying to escape the pain. At that moment, his eyes opened slightly, and "his" face should have been there...

Tomoki arched his back as their lips pressed hard against each other's and "he" pushed in as deeply as he could. "His" movements had become faster and rougher. Tomoki felt a tremor of pleasure race through his entire body. At first he had been afraid of this painful, scary thing, but now he was used to it.

"Remember me. Hurry up and remember..." "He" said between gasps.

"I will," Tomoki answered, clinging onto "his" back desperately. He felt as if his consciousness would be washed away. "XXX!" Tomoki called "his" name between rough, trembling gasps.

"Ohhhhh!" His body arched violently backwards, making the bedsprings bounce. "Ow..." Tomoki had hit his head on the wooden headboard. He had just woken up. He combed his tangled brown hair back and shook his head, dazed.

He sat up in bed and timidly looked inside his pajama pants. "Oh, crap!" he whispered. *Another wet dream.* He couldn't help but feel guilty. Why was he having so many wet dreams lately? Was he touching himself while he was asleep, like some kind of sleepwalking thing? "Damn, my back hurts..." The whole lower half of his body was trembling. He couldn't clearly remember the dream he had just had, but at the very least he knew his partner hadn't been a girl. He couldn't remember his lover's face, but he knew he had

had sex with a man who had a very nice body. A shiver ran down his spine.

This isn't the first time I've had that dream. I think I've had it before...a lot. Did I feel that guy entering me? They say your dreams represent your desires, but then that means I...Does that mean I secretly want to be raped by a guy or something?

"No way..."

As he remembered more of the dream, his face grew red and then pale. "No way...there's no way it's true." He tried to make excuses, and shook his head furiously with tears in his eyes. "Yeah. I probably just fell off my bed in the middle of the night or something." He tried to explain away his back pain, and went to the bathroom to take care of his dirty pajama pants.

Tomoki sat in the classroom before homeroom began. The view of the mid-April sky from the window was clear and blue and the wind that blew in was refreshing. It had been two weeks since he started high school. He didn't know all of his classmates' names yet, but he was relatively happy with his class and the school. He didn't really have any worries.

"I wonder what it all means..." he muttered from his seat by the window. "I just feel so sluggish..." he murmured, putting his head down on his desk. No matter how hard he tried, he just didn't have any energy.

Was it just a regular sex dream like everyone else has during puberty?

Tomoki thought he was pretty much a realist.

So why did he have that flower dream, like he was a princess waiting for her prince to come?

What if I really like guys?!

"Maybe I'm just frustrated..." He tilted his head and sighed. He wished he would have dreams about girls, but for the past two weeks he had had frequent dreams where he was having very realistic sex with another man.

This isn't good...Every time I have a dream about him having sex with me I know I'm actually feeling it.

"Tomo-kun, you look exhausted!" A few of his male classmates came up to him, peering at his face teasingly. They had only been in the same class for two weeks. The only one among them that was able to talk to him with such familiarity was a kid he had gone to middle school with.

"Yeah, I had a bad dream last night," Tomoki answered, still face-down on his desk.

"You poor thing!" The boys said sarcastically, messing up Tomoki's wavy brown hair.

"Knock it off!" Tomoki sulked, putting both hands on his disheveled hair.

"Whatever," his middle school classmate, Tashiro, said. "Hey, do you have the math homework for second hour?"

"Oh, crap!" Tomoki quickly raised his face at Tashiro's request. "Ahh, I forgot it!" His big brown eyes gleamed amber in the sunlight. "I'm screwed!" he said in a pitiful voice, scratching his head. Tomoki was the kind of person whose emotions showed clearly on his face and in his eyes.

"Maybe I should let you borrow my perfect notes?" Tashiro said teasingly, holding out a paper and shaking it around. He was the only person from Tomoki's junior high who was in the same class as him. He was extremely intelligent, and the two of them had only recently become friends.

"Seriously?!" Tomoki held out his hands and his eyes shone bright with expectation. Tashiro looked like he was having a lot of fun at Tomoki's expense. "Thanks! I owe you one," Tomoki said happily as he took the notes in both hands.

"Okay, then maybe you could make it up to me with some, uh, *physical* labor."

"Yeah, just tell me when!" Tomoki said seriously, and the crowd around him erupted with laughter.

"Isn't he hilarious? He's been an airhead like this ever since middle school!" Tashiro said, pointing. Everyone nodded emphatically. Tomoki was 167 centimeters tall, and from his looks alone seemed like he would be popular with the girls, but he was still completely a child.

"It's pretty funny to bully Naruse, isn't it?" Tomoki didn't realize what was going on. He hadn't thought it was bullying. But he was the kind of person who trusted everyone, no matter what.

"Little Tomo-kun still isn't interested in girls, huh?" Tashiro teased.

Tomoki pursed his lips together indignantly. "Actually, I like girls a lot," he countered, and looked at the group of girls across the aisle. They were chattering with each other animatedly, each one cute in her own way. They wore the high school uniform all the neighborhood girls longed to wear—a grey blazer with a red tie and a green tartan miniskirt.

There was a tall boy who stood out among them, standing right in the middle. It was Tomoki's classmate, Yuugo Oda. He was tall and slim, with a fearless, mature face. He had a very strong-sounding name, but his smile was friendly, and he reminded Tomoki of a big, gentle dog.

"Oda's tall, so our uniform looks good on him," he said enviously. In middle school they wore a black uniform with gold buttons. The only thing different about the high school uniform was that it had gold clasps in place of the buttons. The girls' uniforms were cute, but the simplicity of the boys' uniforms looked cool in a different way, depending on who wore them. But those that looked best in them were stylish guys with long legs. Someone tall, with broad shoulders, like Oda.

"He has a nice face, and he's tall, so I guess that's why the girls like him."

"And he's really smart, too." Suddenly the boys around him had started to join in the conversation.

"Every time we have a day off, I heard some older girl goes to his apartment." Their voices started to lower.

"Guess they're on pretty *familiar* terms, huh?"

"Even his name sounds snobby."

"Hey, it's not his fault what his name is!" Tomoki said, feeling bad that this gossip had started because of him.

"Yeah, when you actually get to know him, he's

pretty cool," Tashiro added.

The school bell rang, and the girls around Yuugo went to sit down in their seats. "He's so nice to everyone, but I heard Oda-kun has a girlfriend!"

"A different girl asks him out every day, but he won't go out with any of them!" Some of the girls grumbled as they walked past Tomoki.

"I guess Oda's a good guy after all."

"Yeah, it's pretty rare for a guy our age to be so serious about one girl," Tomoki said as he noticed his friends' attitudes becoming more favorable to Yuugo.

As he walked back to his desk, Tomoki felt someone's eyes on him and turned around. His gaze met Yuugo's. He was sitting at his desk with his head in his hands. They smiled at each other, and Tomoki scratched his head with embarrassment, turning away.

Yuugo Oda, huh...

Their seats were far away from each other, so they didn't have much of an opportunity to talk to each other. But Yuugo had been on his mind since they started school.

"Tomoki, I came to see you." Those were the first words Yuugo had ever said to him. It was right before they had introduced themselves to the class during homeroom, and Tomoki had been startled when the unfamiliar boy had called him by his name. Of course, Tomoki had never met him before. Yuugo had just moved from Shikoku. He had never heard of the town Yuugo had grown up in, and they definitely weren't related. At any rate, Tomoki had never even been to Shikoku.

"Um, who are you?" Tomoki had tilted his head and asked.

Yuugo's eyes had widened with surprise. "You mean you don't remember me?" he had whispered and sighed.

"Have we met somewhere?"

"Just...Never mind."

It had bothered Tomoki so much that he had chased after him and asked again, but Yuugo had just smiled and shook his head.

"Here, Oda-kun," a tan, blonde girl said during a break, handing Yuugo a drink and some candy. He accepted them with a smile, and the other boys in the class looked on with amused expressions on their faces. Tomoki also couldn't help staring at Yuugo, who in turn was staring at the can of soda the girl had given him. He narrowed his eyes.

Maybe he has a thing for that girl? Tomoki wondered.

Yuugo opened the can of soda with a serious look on his face. Tomoki watched as he brought the can to his lips and drank from it. Suddenly Yuugo yelled, "Ahh! There's some kind of foam in my mouth!!"

What?! Tomoki's eyes widened with surprise.

"Is this really a drink?" He pulled the can of soda away from his lips with a disgusted look on his face, and Tomoki noticed the whole class was just as dumbfounded as he was.

"Are you for real, Oda?" a boy nearby said incredulously, which prompted the whole class to join in.

"Don't tell me you've never had soda before!"

"So, what, it's carbonated or something?" Yuugo asked the boys around him, scratching his head.

"Wow, Oda is hilarious! I can't believe him!" Tashiro said, laughing. It seemed that whenever someone as "perfect" as Oda made such a mistake, his likeability factor increased among the other boys.

But it all seemed rather strange to Tomoki. He tilted his head, laughing, and stared at Yuugo, who still had a confused look on his face.

At lunch, Tomoki sat down with Tashiro and his friends. "Pudding tastes good with today's menu."

"Pudding goes good with everything. You really love pudding, huh, Tomo-kun?" Tashiro laughed at Tomoki, who had two containers of pudding on his tray.

"What's wrong with it?" He was about to open a container of pudding when his eyes met Yuugo's, who was just entering the cafeteria. As usual, he was surrounded by girls. Still keeping his gaze on Tomoki, Yuugo waved them off and began to walk alone.

"Can I sit here?" He pointed to an empty seat beside Tomoki, smiling.

"Um, sure..." Tomoki said with a spoonful of pudding in his mouth, his face turning red. Yuugo was undeniably handsome. He had black, almond-shaped eyes that lit up when he smiled.

"What's with that smile? You tryin' to sell us something?"

"Oda, do you seduce guys, too?" The boys at the

table asked seriously. Their chopsticks had all stopped moving, and everyone's faces were bright red. Yuugo's features suggested he might be wild, but his smile was gentle and flirtatious, which sent a shiver down Tomoki's spine.

"What does 'seduce' mean?"

"Oda always smiles like that, right?" Tomoki said convincingly from beside him, trying to defend him.

"Yeah," Yuugo nodded and smiled. "I always smile like this." He stared at Tomoki, who was still holding his pudding container. He felt his cheeks growing hot.

"I bet the girls always misinterpret it, huh?" Tomoki nudged Yuugo, trying to hide his embarrassment.

When they had first met, Yuugo had smiled at Tomoki normally, but up close his smile was very flirtatious. Even though Tomoki knew he was another guy, it made him feel strange inside. It was so enticing; he couldn't tear his eyes away from Yuugo.

"I guess guys can be sexy, too."

"Your smile is so flirty it's embarrassing!"

"Flirty?" Yuugo tilted his head, puzzled at everyone's comments.

"Hey, Oda. Don't tell me you're an airhead like Naruse!"

"Don't you realize when you're hitting on people?"

"Hitting on people? Hey, I'm against violence, guys!" Yuugo said with complete seriousness. Everyone at the table stared at him, amazed.

"...Oda is seriously hilarious."

"If you're that friendly to everyone, people will

start to think you like guys!" As Yuugo and the others exchanged friendly conversation, Tomoki was still confused and absentmindedly started to eat his lunch.

I guess he just smiles at everyone like that... He felt himself get a little disappointed at this.

He had thought he was special, the only one Oda smiled at like that. His eyes had looked so familiar.

But I guess everyone else feels the same way...

"Naruse hasn't been getting very good sleep lately." The boys brought up the subject from earlier that morning.

"Ha ha ha! I guess Tomo-kun's been having some perverted dreams!" Tashiro said after he saw Tomoki blushing. "Don't worry about it. Our bodies get stimulated by every little thing at this age. It's worse when we sleep!"

"Yeah, you can't help it if you dream about having sex with some random businessman or the old lady from the convenience store. Or even a dog or a motorcycle!" Everyone solemnly agreed with Tashiro, but Tomoki tilted his head doubtfully.

"Just be thankful it's not real and just jack off or something. You shouldn't let it built up. I heard that causes pimples."

"So it's okay as long as the person you have sex with is human?" Tomoki asked, confused.

"I dunno, but I heard hot ramen noodles feel really good."

"Yeah, the point is to get something as warm as body temperature."

"What does this have to do with my dreams?"

Tomoki fell on the table, exhausted, and just listened as Tashiro and the other boys talked about sex.

When the bell rang signaling the end of lunch, everyone around him stood up and he heard someone say, "Tomoki." Yuugo had been quiet until that point, but leaned over and whispered his name in his ear, like a secret. "Wanna walk home together today?"

"Okay," Tomoki answered quietly, still lying on the table. He didn't raise his face until after Yuugo had left. He put his hands over his hot ears. He knew his ears and face were probably bright red. His heart thumped wildly in his chest. He felt his whole body responding to the echo of Yuugo's low voice in his head. It felt like he had just been asked out on a date by his crush.

"No, that's not it!" He smacked his own cheeks. "It's just two friends walking home together!" He shook his head, again making up excuses. Oda was friendly to everyone. And everyone misunderstood it as him flirting with them. "He has a problem." A big problem. And that was his sweet voice and smile. "I should warn him... As a friend!" He wasn't exactly sure what he should warn him *about*, but he made up his mind to do so, nevertheless.

After school, Tomoki cheerfully gathered up his belongings.

"Tomoki, can you wait a bit?"

"Sure."

Yuugo was writing in the cleaning log, so Tomoki sat in an empty seat in front of him to wait. Yuugo always addressed him without honorifics, and even Tomoki thought it was strange that the familiarity didn't make him uncomfortable.

"Oda, can I ask you something?" The classroom was almost empty, with only a few of their classmates remaining. "How did you know my name when we first met?" While Tomoki was talking, Yuugo had written something in his notebook and handed it to him.

"It's YUUGO," he read the big letters he had written seriously.

"No, I know your name, Oda..."

"Yuugo!" He pointed to the notebook again.

"C-Can I call you Yuugo?" Tomoki asked helplessly. Yuugo smiled, looking satisfied. "You're so weird." Yuugo had suddenly looked so childish; it made him feel strange.

Many of Yuugo's friends talked to him as they left, and they all called him "Oda," but he seemed not to care. *Does he want only me to call him that?* Tomoki's mood began to improve, so he didn't notice that Yuugo had completely dodged his question.

"About my dreams..." Tomoki said as they walked out of a convenience store they had stopped by on their way home.

"Hmm?" Yuugo looked up as he drank his coffee.

"Do you ever have sex dreams, Yuugo?" he asked hesitantly.

Yuugo smiled cheerfully. "I have *good dreams* all the time, just like you."

"I feel like mine are bad dreams, though."

I'm sure of it!

"Really?"

"Really," Tomoki asserted.

"I have dreams about having sex with a really cute lover." Tomoki was taken aback by Yuugo's frankness.

"That sounds pretty intense. Is it someone you're dating in real life? Your girlfriend?" Even though he was drinking cold orange juice, when Yuugo smiled at him like that, he felt hot. But he couldn't read too much into it. It was just a habit of Yuugo's. "So I guess you've had sex with her in real life."

"No, I've never even held hands with anyone in real life."

"Seriously? So it's a one-sided affair? Even though all the girls want you?" Tomoki asked with surprise.

Yuugo laughed. "It's not *exactly* one-sided. In the dreams, they always have their eyes closed and never even try to look at my face!"

"Like Sleeping Beauty?"

"No, more like even though they're awake they can't face reality, so they won't open their eyes."

"Won't face reality? But it's a dream, right?"

"That doesn't mean it's not real," Yuugo smiled.

Tomoki blinked repeatedly. "I have no idea what you're talking about," he said, exasperated.

"Tomoki."

"What?"

"Doesn't the sex you have in your dreams feel good?" Yuugo suddenly whispered right into his ear. Tomoki was so surprised he dropped the sandwich he had just bought.

"Yuugo!" He exclaimed as he turned bright red and

covered his ears.

Yuugo picked up the sandwich that had come unwrapped and threw it in the garbage can. "Don't get so mad, I'll buy you another one."

"That's not what I mean!"

Yuugo put his arm around him and they went back inside. Only now, Tomoki was bright red with anger.

It was growing dark as they approached the park near Tomoki's house. It was heavily wooded and the streetlights were already glowing blue-white. As he listened to Tomoki chattering on, Yuugo casually looked towards the corner of the park. His eyes quickly narrowed, but he kept the smile on his face. "Impossible..." he whispered in a low voice so Tomoki couldn't hear. Two red lights glowed in the midst of the dark trees. "Why?" He had seen *them* before. But *they* were not supposed to be here.

The red, reptilian eyes were staring at him, waiting for an opportunity. Yuugo stared back harshly, and the two red eyes slowly shifted downward. It was almost like watching a snake slither away on the ground.

"Yuugo, what's wrong?" Tomoki looked up at him, watching as he stared somewhere into the deserted park.

After dinner, Tomoki took a long bath and sighed. The spring nights were still chilly. It was already pitch black outside the small bathroom window. He stretched his fingers out in the warm water and stared at them. Then he thought of Yuugo. "This house with the blue roof is mine," Tomoki had said, pointing to the house right next to the park. "Wanna come in?" He wanted to invite him in, but all Yuugo had said was, "Oh," and then, "Okay, Tomoki. I hope you have good dreams again tonight." He had waved, then started walking down the sidewalk between Tomoki's house and the park. He lived in a brand-new condo complex on the other side of the road, also by the park, about three minutes away.

I didn't know he lived so close..."He's so cold. Well, I guess he's not exactly *cold,* but still..." Tomoki mused as he held onto the sides of the bathtub. He was nice to everyone, so that wasn't really the case. "I guess 'indifferent' is a better word." He splashed his hands into the water, and then yelled, "No wait—that's still not right!" He wanted to describe Yuugo's simple behavior earlier, but he figured there wasn't a word to describe that sort of behavior between men.

Maybe I'm just excited because I want to become closer to him?

He tilted his head. He didn't know why he was feeling so impatient. Yuugo was his classmate; he'd be able to see him again the next morning.

As he dried his wet hair with a towel, Tomoki headed to his room on the second floor. He climbed the stairs then walked down the hallway. There were two rooms there, and his was the room to the right. The one to the left was his older brother's room, but he had died when Tomoki was very young. His parents hadn't touched it since; it was still exactly the way his brother had left it.

It happened when Tomoki was only one year old, so he had no memories of his brother. "Tomo-kun, you look so much like your brother, but your personalities are the exact opposite!" his parents and relatives always used to tell him. Unlike Tomoki, who was lively and mischievous, his brother had been quiet and well-behaved. Sometimes he felt angry at being compared to his late brother. But when he saw the room that wasn't being used, he sometimes thought how fun it might have been had his brother still been alive.

He opened his door and searched for the light switch with his fingers. He felt the hard sensation of the switch, and, just as he was about to turn the lights on, Tomoki casually looked up—and was startled at what he saw.

The silhouette of a human form with large wings was outlined in his dark room. Tomoki only saw it for a split-second before he blinked. He quickly turned on the lights, and the fluorescent light flickered on overhead. Under the bright lights, his room looked completely normal. There was no sign of any disturbance around his window. His blue curtains weren't moving a bit. "What the hell ..." Tomoki decided it must have been some kind of optical illusion, but he remembered how realistic the figure had looked. It was the size of a normal human, but its wings were so large when spread that they barely fit in Tomoki's small bedroom.

"A demon..." He suddenly blurted out the thing that most closely resembled what he had seen before in books and movies. "No, there's no way..." He smiled at his own wild imagination. Suddenly,

Tomoki heard a loud fluttering noise like the beating of wings from the roof. His heart pounded. The sound of wings soon grew quiet, as if whatever it was had flown far away into the night. Tomoki was a little pale and sighed loudly. He switched on the radio near his desk and felt relaxed as the familiar sound of the DJ's voice filled the room.

"Had to be an optical illusion!" Tomoki flopped down on his bed. As he finished drying his hair, he started to feel embarrassed by his fear. He had thought he wasn't the type of person who had dreams a lot, whether it was while he was asleep or even dreams for the future. He thought himself a realist.

But that night, Tomoki slept with the lights on. He had been about to turn the lights off when he remembered the figure he had seen, and chills ran down his spine. "I'm not really scared or anything," he said aloud as he slipped into bed, even though no one was listening. He felt his cheeks grow hot.

It was a moonless night. The houses were all dark and the air was quiet, as if even it had stopped, too. Just before dawn, a faint shadow emerged from the darkness behind Tomoki's house. At the same time, there was a fluttering sound, and from his back he spread two giant wings that were each about two meters long. He quietly glanced around before folding his wings neatly into place. If anyone had seen this mysterious sight, they probably would have screamed. But the owner of the black wings quietly slipped into the night and disappeared like an illusion.

Towards the end of April, Tomoki had adjusted to his new class and formed friendships with a group of his classmates. Some lived near him, and sometimes they would even walk home with Yuugo and Tomoki.

"It's a bit of a detour, but do you want to go check out the new video games there?" Tomoki pointed to a large electronics shop. "Do you play video games, Yuugo? What kind do you like?"

"I've never played any. What kinds of games are there?" Yuugo asked curiously.

Tomoki took him over to the video game section of the store and showed him a few. He was happy when Yuugo seemed enthusiastic to talk about popular CDs, video games, and movies. "Okay, I'll buy some."

"Yeah, let's trade sometime, too!" Tomoki nodded cheerfully. Yuugo started putting all the games Tomoki recommended into his shopping basket. "Yuugo, you need a game console or you can't play those."

"Oh, I'll just buy one, then," he said, heading towards the register.

"But shouldn't you ask your parents first?" Tomoki asked as he followed behind. But Yuugo not only ordered a video game console, but a TV, VCR, and a computer right on the spot. "If you buy all that at once, won't you get in trouble?"

"Nah. I live alone anyway, and I don't have anything in my apartment yet. I just moved in."

He must be pretty rich if he can buy all that with a

credit card, Tomoki thought.

"Oh, yeah—how many TVs should I buy?" Yuugo asked an employee, who, along with Tomoki, stared at him in disbelief.

"Wait a second, one TV is enough!" Tomoki, beginning to get worried, took Yuugo by the arm and led him to the corner of the store. There were a lot of TVs there, each with a different show playing on them. He explained that if you change the channel, the show will change, too. Yuugo seemed genuinely impressed by this.

"Seriously...where the hell did you used to live?"

"I told you, out in the country in Shikoku," Yuugo answered. He really seemed like he had never seen a TV before. Tomoki asked him more questions, and Yuugo seemed to know about newspapers, magazines, and how to work appliances like refrigerators and washing machines.

"Were you from a really poor family or something?"

"Not really. We just didn't have a TV is all," Yuugo said with a smile on his face, but that still didn't ease Tomoki's worries.

"If you're gonna buy something expensive, can you at least ask me about it first?" Tomoki asked with a serious look on his face. He felt like he just couldn't leave Yuugo alone. Yuugo was intelligent and got good grades, but he had never had a carbonated drink. He didn't know anything about mainstream, popular culture. It just didn't make sense. *I need to be with him.* Tomoki was suddenly filled with a sense of duty.

"By the way, are you eating right at home?"

"I'm eating what I like," Yuugo answered with a smile.

Tomoki had even started to worry about his eating habits. Yuugo explained that he was eating things from the nearby convenience store and restaurants. *At least he's not eating anything weird.* "I won't tell anyone about this, so you shouldn't mention it either."

"Okay."

Tomoki figured if their classmates got wind of exactly how oblivious Yuugo was they'd be merciless, so he decided to keep it a secret. He was also secretly happy that he was the only one who knew Yuugo so well. Every time they saw each other at school, Tomoki would ask, "How are your studies going?"

"Good," Yuugo would answer with a smile. His "studies" were of TV, games, and other popular, mainstream things. After about a week of this, he became more like a regular high school student. Thanks to the TV and the computer, he was usually able to keep up with normal conversation.

"If you have any questions, just ask me."

"Thanks for helping me so much, Tomoki." Yuugo was always overly impressed by Tomoki's knowledge.

Tomoki thought it was fun recommending his favorite CDs, and they'd often go shopping together. At school, the two became inseparable. Yuugo wasn't that close to anyone else, and he hadn't joined any clubs yet.

I have to stay near him. He needs me! I want to be his best friend. We have so much fun together. He's so unique...and so charming. But maybe everyone else thinks that, too...

"Is Oda in this class?" During breaks, girls from other classes or people recruiting for their clubs would always come to talk to Yuugo. Each time it happened, he would stand and talk to them in the doorway. At the end of April, most everyone in class had decided on a club activity. Since Yuugo was so tall, members of sports clubs always invited him to join, but he hadn't accepted any offers yet.

"I'm Majima from the volleyball club. If you haven't decided on a club activity yet..." And each time Yuugo would stare at them with that smile on his face, and both girls *and* boys were always speechless. His almond-shaped eyes could make anyone's heart pound.

"Yuugo." Tomoki clapped a hand on his shoulder from behind. "I told you, you shouldn't stare at people you don't know like that!" Besides looking after him, Tomoki had recently started scolding him. "Don't pay attention to him, Senpai. He has this habit of staring at people like that. It doesn't mean anything." Even though Tomoki would explain that, they would always hurry away with their faces bright red.

"If you're not trying to come on to them, you shouldn't stare at people like that! It's like you've never seen a face before!" His tone grew a little angry. Even Tomoki would feel his heart pound when Yuugo looked at him like that. As soon as he found out that it was just a habit, he had secretly felt disappointed. And he also felt a little uncomfortable at the same time.

Ever since the incident at the electronics store, Tomoki had felt like he just couldn't leave Yuugo alone, so he had been going around making sure others wouldn't misunderstand Yuugo's behavior.

"Isn't it weird how people have so many different faces?"

Tomoki guessed Yuugo meant it was interesting how different people looked. "Did you not grow up around a lot of people?"

"Yeah, there weren't many people there."

"What, were you raised by wolves in the mountains of Shikoku or something? There are still people out in the country!"

"Wolves? Hmm...Something like that. Anyway, there weren't a lot of people around." Yuugo smiled and lightly stroked Tomoki's hair, like he was petting a cat's fur. "Have you remembered me yet?"

"Remembered what about you?"

"Never mind."

"You are so weird." Tomoki looked away with a fed-up expression on his face. Even though Yuugo had touched him in such a meaningful way, he had still evaded Tomoki's question, as usual. And even though he was growing used to it, Tomoki still blushed furiously when Yuugo got so close to his face.

When he walked around with Yuugo, girls would always come up to them, saying, "Oda-kun!" When they were on their way back from gym after fourth period, girls called out and waved to him. "Over here, Oda-san!" Every time someone called his name, Yuugo would turn towards them and give them his signature smile. Tomoki was obviously annoyed, and walked right past the girls.

"Do you have to be so friendly to everyone?" he asked crossly when they were alone in the locker room. A breeze drifted in from the tall, open window on one side of the room. "You don't have to smile at every single one of them, you know."

"It's not like it's hurting you, right?" Yuugo said as he leaned against the lockers and looked at Tomoki.

"I-I know, but if your girlfriend lived nearby and found out, I bet she'd be really jealous."

"She lives really close," Yuugo answered, smiling.

"What? She's not from Shikoku? I totally thought you were in a long-distance relationship!"

"Nope, the person I love lives here. That's why I moved."

"Don't tell me she's older and you guys live together in your condo or something!" Tomoki's eyes suddenly widened and he leaned in closer. Even though they walked home from school together, Tomoki would always end up going home first.

"Hey, we're the same age and we don't live together."

"Hmm. Really? You walk home with me, so I guess she goes to a different school, huh? What is she like? I bet she's way hotter than the girls at our school." Tomoki was speaking casually, but inside his heart was pounding. "Does she come to your house a lot?" he asked, suddenly feeling nervous.

Maybe that's why he's never invited me inside.

"I see her all the time, but she never comes over. I told you, I've never even held hands before."

"Seriously? She won't even let you hold her hand? She must be a prude," Tomoki said sympathetically. Once he knew Yuugo's girlfriend wasn't going over to his house, Tomoki felt a little relieved. Still, Yuugo had someone he really cared about. *Maybe Yuugo goes home alone so he can change to go out on dates with her...* "Anyway, you should stop smiling like that at everyone you see. For your girlfriend's sake," he said, choosing his words carefully. "If you guys are going out, she probably wants to feel like she's the only special one in your life."

"It sounds like you're jealous or something," Yuugo said, smiling, and Tomoki immediately blushed. "Are you really that worried about me?" He peered at Tomoki's face, amused. "Do you want to get to know me better?"

"Huh?" Tomoki's heart jumped at the tender tone in Yuugo's voice.

"That's why you were waiting for me, right?"

"I..." Tomoki couldn't find the words to answer. He tried to stop himself from blushing at the sensual way Yuugo was staring at him. It was true. He had waited for Yuugo after the bell rang. But that was all. He wasn't jealous, or worried about him, or anything. He wanted to say that, but just couldn't find the words. *Why can't I say anything?* "I-I'm gonna go ahead back to the classroom now," he said quietly as he looked away. *I'm such an idiot.* No matter what Yuugo said to him, he couldn't explain himself. Tomoki was so embarrassed—he had to get out of there.

"I'm sorry, Tomoki." Yuugo grabbed his arm

and pulled him back. "I'll hurry and change, just wait for me," he whispered into his ear. His shirt was still unbuttoned. Tomoki felt the hairs on the back of his neck stand up.

Just then, the bell for lunch rang. Tomoki felt relieved. He pushed on Yuugo's chest. "Hurry up." He grabbed Yuugo's uniform, and they walked out of the locker room even though Yuugo's shirt was still unbuttoned. He began to button it up on the way to the classroom, and was putting on his uniform when some girls called out to him, and he smiled back at them warmly.

He never learns! As Tomoki walked back to his seat, his head began to hurt. Of course it was Yuugo's prerogative to smile, but every time he did so, it irritated Tomoki to no end. He had no idea why. *Maybe it's because I'm jealous that he gets all the attention...or maybe I just want to monopolize him...or maybe I'm just being childish.*

"Can we go home now, Tomoki?" Yuugo called out to him after school.

"Yeah."

He had been in a bad mood, but Tomoki felt himself nodding cheerfully as he picked up his bag. No matter how many cute girls invited him to walk home together, Yuugo would always smile and turn them down, then go over to Tomoki. It definitely made him feel good, but Tomoki was always surprised at the jealous glares from the girls.

"Oh, Tomo-kun!"

"Oda, Naruse will take care of it, so don't flirt with the girls anymore!" Ever since Oda became closer with Tomoki's group of friends, they started teasing him like that. Yuugo gave them a friendly wave and then pushed Tomoki's back.

"Ohhh, looks like Naruse really likes Oda!" Their classmates laughed after the two boys had left the room. Even though his flirtatious smile hadn't changed, Oda had stopped hanging out with the girls so much.

"Guess we finally have a chance with the girls now!" Tashiro said, his eyeglasses gleaming. They had found out that Yuugo was the type of guy who paid no attention to anyone but the person he liked. After a while, the girls would give up on him and start paying attention to the other boys in the class. If that happened, Tashiro and the other boys thought they would definitely get a chance with the girls.

It was a leisurely fifteen minute walk to Tomoki's house from school. A lot of students took the bus, so they didn't usually see many of their classmates walking around nearby. When they entered the residential district from the main street, cars and other passersby were also a rare sight.

"I understand you less and less each day," Tomoki quietly grumbled.

Yuugo laughed and shrugged his shoulders.

"The reason I'm so friendly to everyone is because I don't want to cause conflict. My grandma gave me that advice in her will."

"Oh, come on. I bet your grandma's still alive," Tomoki said in a teasing voice, clapping Yuugo on the shoulder.

Yuugo smiled. "No, I'm serious. It's true. I'm actually not good at getting along with people. I'm just not interested in others."

"Are you for real? Then, why are you going home with me?!"

"Do you not like it?" Yuugo raised his eyebrows.

"That's not what I mean. I was just wondering." When he thought about it, their houses were in the same direction, and Tomoki figured being constantly asked by the girls was annoying, so maybe Yuugo was just walking home with him so he could give them an excuse of "I'm going home with Tomoki." *What exactly do I want him to say?*

Yuugo leaned in and whispered, "As long as you don't have a problem with it, who cares?"

Tomoki held his ears and indignantly cried, "Will you stop whispering in my ears like that?" He turned bright red and showed his irritation to Yuugo, who had an amused look on his face. "You just do this kind of thing to everyone!"

"Have you ever seen me whisper to anyone else?" Yuugo crinkled his eyes and smiled.

I guess not...but...

Tomoki wasn't sure why he was the only one. "Yuugo, are you teasing me?"

"Nah, but you've always liked having your ears touched."

"What are you talking about?!" Tomoki stopped

walking and demanded seriously, but Yuugo kept smiling and pushed him forward.

"We're in the middle of the road, silly." The stoplight was about to turn red, so Tomoki started to run to the other side. "So, where should we go today?"

"You always dodge my questions like that," Tomoki said with a serious face as Yuugo put his arm around his shoulders. "Don't you want to answer anything I ask you?" Yuugo was still so mysterious to him. The more he got to know him, the less he understood him. He thought Yuugo probably liked him, which was why they were friends. But even though he was very friendly, Yuugo didn't talk much. Even though they had been friends for a while, Tomoki had never heard about Yuugo's family or private life.

"Do you just want someone to tease until you have to go home or something?" *Why am I getting so upset?* Among their classmates, Yuugo and Tomoki lived closest to each other. Even if they walked slowly, their houses were only about five minutes apart. They would walk together until the park, then Yuugo would always say, "See ya!" and they would part. "We live so close, but you always go home right away..." His voice sounded so critical, Tomoki clapped his hand over his mouth. He looked down as he felt his face grow hot. "Forget I said that," he said, waving his hands. He didn't want to sound selfish and like he wanted to spend more time with Yuugo.

"Tomoki, do you wanna come over?" Yuugo asked quietly, placing a hand on his shoulder. "Don't get your hopes up. I don't have a lot of stuff yet, so it's a pretty boring place. If that's okay with you, why don't you come over?" His face grew serious, and his usual smile was gone.

Tomoki felt bad about sounding so selfish before, but then felt relieved by Yuugo's request. He started to feel happy. Maybe Yuugo's room had just been messy and he was embarrassed to have him over.

"I live alone, so there's really nothing in there," Yuugo repeated, and Tomoki nodded, his eyes wide.

"You're right...there's really nothing in here," Tomoki whispered as he looked around Yuugo's room.

Yuugo had entered a pass code at the entrance of the building, and then they rode a large elevator up to his room. Even though Yuugo had told him not to get his hopes up, Tomoki was imagining a luxurious condo. It was newly built, so the rooms were clean, and it was large for someone to live in alone. But the three rooms were completely empty. He had the bare necessities, but it didn't feel like someone lived there. There was a narrow bed in the corner of the large living room, and on the opposite side were the computer and television Yuugo had bought with Tomoki, still lying on the floor.

"So, I guess your girlfriend really doesn't come over, huh?" Tomoki felt strangely relieved.

There wasn't a table, so Yuugo set the plastic bags from the convenience store directly on the floor. In the large, empty room, the sound of him rummaging in the bags to get out the drinks they had bought seemed strangely loud. Their voices also echoed, so they both spoke very quietly.

"I think it would be more convenient if you had some furniture here."

"Will you pick some out for me, Tomoki?"

"Okay."

He was living in this nice condo, so it seemed like a pity that he had no furniture. Yuugo was just using the living room and the kitchen; it almost seemed like he was only living there temporarily. The room was warm from the heater, yet Tomoki felt strangely cold. He sat down and hugged his knees to his chest.

Seeing this, Yuugo handed him a down comforter. "Well, I'm not that cold." It was almost as if it wasn't Tomoki's body that was cold, but the atmosphere of the empty room. "So you really live alone, huh, Yuugo?"

"My grandma was the only family I had. She died about two years ago."

"I'm sorry. It was true what you said about your grandma..." Tomoki apologized. He had thought Yuugo was just teasing when he had talked about his grandma's will.

"It's okay, don't worry about it. My dad died when I was really little, and then my mom left and has another family somewhere. I think that kind of thing happens a lot nowadays."

He went on to explain that he had lived with just his grandmother in the country, and while they had a few servants for as long as he could remember who fixed meals and such for them, they had rarely talked to Yuugo. He had taken correspondence courses, and an older man had come to tutor him, as well. He hadn't been outside of his house much since he was about five years old. His grandmother was from a well-known, wealthy family, so the family doctor would come to make house calls. So he never even left the house for medical treatment.

"I was studying at home until last year, so I had never even been inside a school. I've seriously never been around other kids my age. It's the first time I've gone to school, so I can't help it if people think I'm weird. My grandma really did give me that advice in her will. She called it 'the secret to success in life.' No one feels ill will or doubts towards someone who always has a smile on their face, right? If you smile, things will go well."

"I see..." Tomoki looked a little depressed after hearing how Yuugo grew up.

"It's not a big deal," Yuugo said, waving his hand. "So anyway, I just don't understand girls. I only understand about half of what they're saying."

"You're not alone. Girls always talk in abbreviations and stuff, so even the rest of us guys barely understand them."

"Yeah, I bet half the stuff they say isn't even in the dictionary!" Yuugo said, laughing.

Even though Yuugo was laughing, Tomoki couldn't help thinking about how Yuugo was all alone, with no parents or grandmother. He didn't want to blurt out something that sounded like he pitied him. Tomoki couldn't imagine what it must be like to live alone.

"But I like living alone. I don't get my inheritance until I'm twenty, but the person who handles my grandmother's estate, my guardian, bought this condo for me, so I don't have to worry about money. If you're okay with an empty room like this, you should come over more often. But don't tell anyone about it, because I'm not really very good at talking to other people."

"It's okay if I come over? I won't be bothering you?"

"No, you're always welcome here."

Tomoki put his hands on his flushed cheeks and tried not to smile. He was happy that Yuugo shared his secrets with him. As he gazed out the dark window, even the bare floor started to feel warm. "My older brother died in an accident at the beach when he was nine. I was only one, so even if I look at pictures of him, I can't remember him," he said quietly as he and Yuugo sat close together.

His family had gone on a trip to the beach, and, as it was getting dark, his parents had started to gather up their things and had just taken their eyes off his brother for a second when he was swept away by the ocean currents. They never found his body. Tomoki's parents told him the only thing they found of his brother was one of his sandals that had washed up on the beach.

Of course, Tomoki himself didn't remember a thing. When he was young, he thought his "older brother's" room was interesting and he often went in there to play. But as he passed the age his brother had been when he died, it was weird seeing pictures of his older brother looking younger than Tomoki and seeing the elementary school textbooks still in his desk drawers.

"I don't remember anything, so it's not like I'm sad. Sometimes, I wonder what it would be like if he were still alive. But anyway, I wanna hear more about you." Yuugo had placed his hand on Tomoki's shoulder as if to comfort him, so Tomoki tried to quickly change the subject.

"I want to hear about the dreams you've had lately," Yuugo said.

"What do you mean?"

"Didn't you say you had a bunch of sex dreams?"

"Y-Yeah..." Tomoki stammered, surprised at the sudden change of topic.

"I waited all this time, but you still can't remember, huh? I guess drastic times call for drastic measures," Yuugo muttered, as if he was talking to himself.

"Sometimes you say the weirdest stuff. Did we meet a long time ago or something?"

Yuugo put his arm around Tomoki's shoulders and drew him closer. "Think very carefully about why you're so drawn to me."

Tomoki's head swam as he grew strangely conscious of how Yuugo's shirt was unbuttoned at the top, his chest exposed.

"And maybe you'll have 'sweet dreams' tonight," Yuugo said with his sensual smile.

"I just don't get Yuugo..." Tomoki said to himself as he sat down on his bed. He had been shocked at how closely Yuugo had held him, but even more so at what he had said next. *"I only have one bed."* He had said it so meaningfully.

Tomoki had thought Yuugo was going to kiss him

or something. He thought that, as a friend, he should look him in the eyes and refuse, but he knew he wouldn't be able to speak if he looked into those eyes. His heart had pounded, and Tomoki had felt his face getting hot. He started to doubt even himself. If Yuugo really pursued him, what would he do? What *should* he do? His mind raced. But then Yuugo had said, "You should probably go home now," and stood up, smiling. Then he had walked Tomoki back out to the entrance of the building.

What was that about?! How does he feel about me? Tomoki shouted silently. If Yuugo had asked "Do you wanna sleep together?" Tomoki was pretty sure he'd have mustered up the strength to run away. Yuugo was probably just teasing him again. That had to be it. But if it wasn't, Tomoki was in trouble...

As he lay in bed, Tomoki put his hand over his chest and could feel his heart racing. *How do I feel about Yuugo?* As he worried about that, his eyelids grew heavy and he dozed off, falling into a deep, deep sleep. It was so deep that when he woke up in the morning he didn't remember anything about how he fell deep into dreams.

He fell down slowly, like a feather. Someone had caught his arm to steady his body. Even though his eyes were still closed, he felt relieved and smiled at the strong feeling on his arm. The sweet scent of flowers drifted in the air.

"Why don't you remember me?" Someone whispered into his ear in the dream. "Why don't you open your eyes, Tomoki? Don't you want to recognize me?" He only realized it was "him" after hearing his own name. It was a familiar voice. He felt like he had heard the owner of the voice say that line many times before. In his half-conscious state, he recognized that he was dreaming. But in the dream, Tomoki's eyes were closed. "Are you afraid I'll look like a monster?" the man said uneasily.

Tomoki felt himself shake his head. "No, that's not it," he said, his eyes still closed. He knew he had probably never thought the man was scary. "I'm so tired." He felt the warmth of the other man's body holding him, and grew sleepy from the comfort of it.

The man kissed him, and as Tomoki answered the moist feeling of his tongue, he wrapped his arms around the man's strong body. He melted against the man's warm chest and under his kisses. He felt rough kisses along the nape of his neck, and his closed eyelids trembled as his face winced with pain. "That hurts, XXX!" Tomoki called the man's name and tried to resist a little. But his body grew hot from the man's skillful fingers. He started panting under the man's warm body.

"Listen...when you wake up, look at the marks I made on you in the mirror. And then say my name out loud..."

"Oh...kay..." Tomoki answered, panting. He clung to the man's sweaty body.

Before dawn, Tomoki opened his eyes and jumped up in bed. "No way..." His body felt like it had just had sex, and he gulped as he looked down at his disheveled pajamas. He went to the bathroom quietly, so that he wouldn't wake his parents. Turning on the light, Tomoki timidly unbuttoned his pajama top. There were bright red hickeys on his neck. Not only that, but there were faint bite marks and more hickeys here and there around his nipples. He was dumbfounded. "Yuugo..." he said unconsciously. He was astonished at the name he had just whispered.

Tomoki was restless all morning. He couldn't help but think about Yuugo, who sat in his seat near the doorway. Maybe he had just been thinking of him since they had such a private conversation at his place, and that's why he had said his name? When Tomoki thought of the events that took place between the previous night and that morning, he felt like he had definitely had a dream. Then he remembered—a dream about having sex with his friend...Yuugo. *I'm such an idiot!* He wanted to scream out loud, but it was a dream so it wasn't like he could control it. It was a dream, but ... *Why do I have those bite marks and those hickeys?!* There was no way he could have given them to himself!

"Listen...when you wake, look at the marks I made on you in the mirror. And then say my name out loud..." "he" had said in Tomoki's dream. The man who always had sex with him in his dreams. So why had he said Yuugo's name? He wanted to think it was because they spent so much time together. It made him want not to talk to Yuugo that day.

Is the guy from my dreams really Yuugo? Do I love him and want to have sex with him? No, just calm down!

Tomoki's head was spinning. The problem here

wasn't if he loved another man. It was that the things that happened in his dreams seemed to be happening in reality.

He was afraid that he had started to believe something very unrealistic. Tomoki spent the whole day at school a nervous wreck. In order to avoid talking to Yuugo, he left the classroom on breaks, and sat hunched over during class. They hadn't even made eye contact until after school was over, but Yuugo made no effort to come talk to him. So when Yuugo left the classroom alone, Tomoki flopped down on his desk and sighed loudly.

When Tomoki opened his eyes in the classroom, it was already getting dark outside. From the window he could see that the setting sun was changing the sky from red to purple, making the familiar classroom seem cold. "Did I fall asleep?" he murmured as he stared at the chalkboard. There didn't seem to be anyone left in the dark hallways. Tomoki felt uneasy at being left all alone, and began to tremble. Even though it was May, it was still chilly, and he started to wish he had brought a jacket to school that day. He didn't think his classmates were so mean as to leave him sleeping there alone ...

Tomoki began to feel uneasy as the purple sky took on a blue tint, like the witching hour was approaching. The outlines of the desks and chairs began to become indistinct. Even when he strained his eyes, he couldn't make out their forms. The darkness began to feel ominous. Tomoki couldn't bear it any longer, grabbed his bag and stood up.

"Are you going home by yourself?" Tomoki jumped at the sudden sound of a voice coming from behind him. When he turned around, his heart pounded as he saw someone sitting in a desk wearing black clothes, alone in the darkness.

"Yuugo?" It took him a while to realize who it was. Tomoki knew even his fingers were trembling as he held his bag. He wished there was some kind of light on. What had he been doing in this dark room, not saying a word?

"It's dark outside, now. It's dangerous, so I'll walk you home," Yuugo said. Tomoki couldn't see his face in the dark.

"Yuugo, why are you still here?" Tomoki finally got up the courage to ask when they neared the shoe lockers. The lights there were still on.

"Watching," Yuugo said nonchalantly as he changed his shoes.

"Watching what?" Tomoki asked curiously, led on by a false sense of security at the normalcy of Yuugo's voice. "I wish you would have woken me up before it got dark. By the way, have you decided on a club yet? If not, you should soon. You like sports, right?" Tomoki kept chattering on, almost like he was afraid of silence.

They went out the school gates. Even though the road was lit by streetlights, Tomoki felt like it was unusually dark that night. He was glad he didn't have to walk home by himself.

"So what were you watching?"

"Everything getting dark around you."

"What?" For a second, Tomoki had forgotten what he had even asked him, and suddenly got goosebumps. He felt like the air around them had grown cold, and unconsciously crossed his arms. "What does that mean? You always talk weird, so I misunderstand you a lot. You weren't watching me, so what were you watching?" He tried to sound teasing, but he couldn't hide his trembling voice.

"I told you, I was watching everything getting dark around you," Yuugo repeated slowly. The hair on the back of Tomoki's neck stood up.

"Yuugo, explain it so I can understand," Tomoki said, again trying to sound cheerful. He found himself backing away slowly.

"Tomoki, did you look in the mirror this morning like you were supposed to?" As Yuugo said this, he reached out his hand and unfastened the clasp on Tomoki's collar. "He" touched a hickey with his finger. "You said my name, didn't you?"

"H-How did you...?!"

"You remembered everything, didn't you?"

Tomoki looked down and nodded, which made Yuugo smile gently. "I see. I'm glad you remembered. I was worried that once you met me *in Reality*, you'd fall asleep too fast in your dreams."

Fall asleep in my dreams? Tomoki replayed Yuugo's words over and over again in his mind. Of course he would be sleeping when he was dreaming, but he felt like that wasn't what Yuugo had meant.

"You didn't want to admit in Reality that I was making love to you, right?"

"Making lo— Hey, wait a second!" Tomoki said as he heard the truth he had feared.

"I was only able to stay human because I met you in your dreams." Yuugo looked down at him as they walked along the dark road on their way home. Tomoki couldn't believe Yuugo was a bad guy when he saw the kindness in his eyes.

"I...don't understand what you mean by that," Tomoki said hesitantly. "I'm sorry, but I don't remember my dreams." It was half-truth, half-lie. He didn't know if the strange things he had experienced lately were because of Yuugo or not.

Tomoki's house was on the edge of the residential district across from the park which was already lit by the blue-white glow of the streetlights. He and Yuugo slowly walked side by side. Tomoki could see the lights on inside his house. His mother was probably making dinner and waiting for him. He found himself unable to believe that he was walking together with Yuugo on that dark road. But what exactly couldn't he believe? He didn't know, himself. That Yuugo was a normal human being? Or that he was the same person that Tomoki made love to in his dreams?

He didn't understand the meaning of what Yuugo had said about being able to "stay human." If he wasn't human, then what was he? Tomoki's mind raced. They neared his house, and suddenly Yuugo silently turned the corner of the dark alley.

"Hey, wait a second!" Tomoki cried towards Yuugo. "Why are you going home so quickly? I don't understand anything that's just happened!"

"Why are you stopping me?" Yuugo said quietly, still not turning around. It was the first time Tomoki had ever heard irritation in his voice.

"Because...I just can't accept things the way they...are..." he trailed off. He didn't know what he couldn't accept or why he had stopped Yuugo, either.

"Do you really want to believe me?" Yuugo turned around slowly and stared at Tomoki. There was no smile on his face. Tomoki's chest tightened, as it was the first time he'd ever seen such a cold expression on Yuugo's face.

He was sure this was Yuugo's true face, when he wasn't putting on a fake smile to please people. His eyes were coldly indifferent.

It was almost as if he was about to say, "I have no use for you anymore," and Tomoki suddenly found it hard to breathe. Until then, he had thought that Yuugo thought he was special.

"I was only able to stay human because I met you in your dreams."

There was no way that the smile Yuugo had given when he had said that so tenderly was false. Tomoki suddenly felt like he was about to cry. He clenched his fists and looked up. "I'll listen to whatever you have to say." He felt that if they parted like this, he would never see Yuugo's smile again. "So just explain it in a way that's easy for me to understand!"

Tomoki put down his bag in the foyer and explained to his mother that he'd be home late. He saw Yuugo greet his mother behind him, and his face was all smiles, just like normal. Tomoki felt relieved. His mother also seemed relieved that Tomoki had a "friend" that lived so close to them. "Are you sure your friend doesn't want to join us for dinner, Tomoki?"

"Thank you. Maybe next time," Yuugo politely declined Tomoki's mother's invitation.

"Yuugo, are you sure we can't talk inside?" The two of them began to walk along the sidewalk by the park. On their right was the dimly lit park and to their left were the mortar bricks of rows of houses. "You should have at least come in for dinner."

"You're lucky to have a family."

"What?" Tomoki looked up at the sound of self-derision in Yuugo's voice.

"We're the same, but why are our environments so different? Is it because you've been so slow to 'awaken'?" he murmured, sighing. "It's not fair." Yuugo brushed his hair back and stared at Tomoki.

"Yuugo?"

Suddenly, Yuugo put his right hand on the bricks and grabbed Tomoki. The streetlights from the park did not illuminate them. Light and darkness were clearly defined. Tomoki tried to retreat back into the light, but Yuugo wouldn't let his hand go. He couldn't see Yuugo clearly in the shadows; the only thing still illuminated by the blue-white light was half of Yuugo's face. He was smiling, as usual.

"It's not fair. You and I are the same... We make love all the time, but when you wake you act like it was only a dream."

"Yuugo!" Tomoki raised his voice, and Yuugo briefly let go of his hand. He stretched it out in front of him. It cast a dark shadow on Tomoki's face.

"Listen. You and I are the same." Yuugo slowly brought his hand next to Tomoki. When Tomoki looked at it, a shiver went down his spine. Even though there was supposed to have been a brick wall next to him, Yuugo's hand had penetrated it with no resistance.

Why?! The color drained from Tomoki's face as if he had just seen a ghost. He desperately tried to push Yuugo away, but just ended up tripping backwards. "What?" The sensation of the brick wall that he had been pressing his back up against was now gone. Tomoki's figure was swallowed up by the darkness, as if he had fallen off a cliff.

"Ahhhhhh!!"

Tomoki felt an overwhelming sensation of vertigo, as if he were actually falling off a cliff. He screamed as he clutched fearfully at Yuugo. *I'm gonna die!* He saw the ground approaching, then squeezed his eyes shut. Before long, they would crash into the hard earth and his bones would be crushed. *I'm gonna die, and it's going to be all Yuugo's fault!* At that moment, a black flame burst forth. Giant wings spread from Yuugo's back.

Each one had to be at least three meters wide when he spread them. The jet black wings that sprouted through his school uniform made a loud rustling noise. They vigorously flapped two, then three times. Their bodies, which had been falling, now lightly floated in mid-air. The force of the wings had brought them upright again, and they both touched the ground with their feet at the same time, with Tomoki still holding onto Yuugo.

It took a long time for Tomoki to realize that he was now standing on the ground. He blinked repeatedly and then raised his face, timidly looking at Yuugo. Tomoki thought Yuugo had transformed into some kind of ghost or demon or something. "That was the first time you fell directly into the darkness, right? Were you scared?" Yuugo asked with a calm expression on his face.

Tomoki nodded.

"We fell into the realm of humans' dreams with our bodies intact. Once you get used to it, as long as there is darkness you can travel through it to reach the Depths of Dreams. It's rare for humans to have this power," Yuugo explained, but Tomoki had a hard time understanding him.

"Wait...Yuugo...you have wings coming from your back!!" He looked up at the wings that were folded against Yuugo's school uniform with a shocked look on his face. They were wings the color of darkness, like a raven's. Up close, the feathers had a beautiful rainbow sheen to them. Several of them had fallen to the ground, and just one of them was about fifteen centimeters long. Tomoki started to panic. "Where are we?"

He looked around wildly. As he strained his eyes in the darkness, Tomoki saw a desolate landscape with rocky cliffs pushing up here and there. It was ominous, like something was lurking in every shadow, and he couldn't calm himself down. Yuugo explained again slowly, and Tomoki shook his head, his eyes still wide. "So we fell into a dream? So, in other words...this is really happening? It's reality?"

"Do you believe it?"

"I'm...not sure."

Maybe he had suddenly lost consciousness by the park or something. Tomoki pinched his cheeks hard. Tears welled up in his eyes from the definite sensation of pain he felt.

"This is a lower strata than the dreams human have," an archaic-sounding voice said by his ear. He heard the sound of wings flapping. Tomoki felt a weight on his shoulder, and saw that a crow was perched on him. "And if you go even lower, you will find the place where Yuugo saved Lord Tomoki."

"Is that a crow?" Tomoki pointed timidly to the bird on his shoulder and asked a smiling Yuugo.

"This place is close to the Underworld, so the demons here are strong. If Yuugo hadn't found you, you would have been eaten alive!" Tomoki suddenly jumped up at the soft sensation he felt coiling around his feet. "How rude! Don't you remember me?" Tomoki blinked at the green eyes that looked up at him from the ground.

"This...is a cat, right?" He had a look of disbelief on his face, and pointed to the cat with golden fur that was standing by Yuugo's feet. Its long tail was divided in two.

"Yuugo, has Lord Tomoki forgotten all about us?" The crow flew over to rest on Yuugo's shoulder and whispered in his ear, hiding his beak behind a wing. But he spoke loudly, so Tomoki could hear everything.

"I helped save Tomoki, too. My name is Jade. Don't you remember?"

"I don't remember...but that's a nice name."

"Uh-huh. My first master gave it to me. He said the color of my eyes was the color of a gem called 'jade,'" the cat proudly proclaimed. "Human Dark Walkers are always males, but I'm a girl. My first two masters died of old age, so everyone started to call me mean names like 'monster.' I got lost once in this world, so I haven't been able to go back to the human world," Jade explained in a bored-sounding voice. She seemed more interested in grooming her golden fur than talking. By all appearances, she seemed like a normal long-haired cat.

"And I!" The crow hurriedly flew back to Tomoki's shoulder. Both his movements and speech were unbelievably fast for a crow. "I am Kurou Myo Ohoyoshimasa. I am a crow *yaksha,* a Buddhist guardian. I used to be a very important *tengu*, but since Yuugo defeated me and stole my beautiful black wings, I lost my powers and became a lowly crow. Not only that, but I am Yuugo's slave! One day, though, I'll get my wings and my powers back!" The crow yelled into Tomoki's ears, which made him squeeze his eyes shut and hold his hands over them.

"Shut up, you loud crow," Yuugo smacked Kurou's head from behind, and the crow tumbled onto the ground.

"You better watch it! I am a *yaksha*!" The bird quickly righted himself beside Jade and pointed one wing at Yuugo, complaining the entire time. "The power of your beautiful wings is *mine!* They are mine! I am just waiting for my chance..."

"Yeah, yeah. Do whatever you want," Yuugo said,

waving his hand.

"He's such a stupid crow, isn't he?" Jade said in an exasperated tone, and smiled with her proud cat face.

It was true that if he talked this loud, Kurou's "chance" would probably never come.

"But Kurou, you're so stupid that Yuugo didn't even think it was necessary to kill you. If he was able to steal your wings, that must mean he was just as strong as you —so maybe you have a problem with intelligence..."

"Why, you rude little—!"

"You don't look strong, so that's why Yuugo decided to fight you. If you let your powers be absorbed you might become a demon, so even Yuugo tries to avoid fighting. I'd be so upset if he got turned into a demon. He's so handsome..."

Listening to Jade and Kurou's exchange, Tomoki was unsure of what he could and could not laugh at.

A cat and a crow were already talking, so he didn't even care anymore. And even Yuugo, who stood next to him, had two giant wings coming from his back.

"But I am glad you have finally awakened. Yuugo hid you somewhere safe every day. This violent man only treats Lord Tomoki with affection."

"That's right! Because of Tomoki, we've been able to approach Yuugo. Until he found you, he was even scarier than demons!"

"I thought Yuugo *was* a demon or a monster!" Jade and Kurou both giggled.

It seemed that not only were there demons in this world, but monsters, too.

"Well, Tomoki? Do you believe me now?"

"Yeah...This is all a dream, right?" Tomoki grabbed Yuugo's arm with an uneasy expression, as if he was searching for answers.

"If only it was as simple as a dream," Yuugo said, and picked Tomoki up in his arms. He spread his wings out and kicked off from the ground. With just a few flaps of his wings, they were high in the air. Jade and Kurou had grown small, and he saw them looking up towards them. Tomoki stared in amazement at the scenery below as he clutched onto Yuugo and they flew through the air. Sometimes there were large mountains and rivers, sometimes deep forests, and sometimes moonlit oceans. The scenery kept changing in a huge panorama.

Each time the scenery changed, it was like they broke through a thin membrane that separated each dream's landscape. "These are the dreams of holy people. There's no safer place than here. Isn't it beautiful?" Yuugo asked, and it seemed like he had wanted to show Tomoki this beautiful place that he had found. Apparently dreams that normal humans had were more abstract and dangerous.

"Is this the landscape of dreams you have at night?"

"Not always." Yuugo touched down on a green hill. In the middle of this beautiful scenery that almost looked like a watercolor painting, there was a small house with a red roof. There was a peaceful looking young man and woman sitting on the lawn in front of it. "There are things that don't change, even if you're not sleeping. This is someone's imagined existence."

Tomoki tried to walk towards them, but for some reason could never get near the house or the couple he could see.

"This place will be peaceful until these people die. It's probably some kind of cherished memory they have together. It's something very close to a supernatural power, but these people are probably living normally somewhere."

Tomoki began to feel even more confused by this strange landscape.

This is the place people go when they sleep. And it's also the place where dreams are created. "We can fall down to the lower strata. It's the place closest to the Underworld, called the 'Depths of Dreams.'" They returned to the bleak landscape of the Depths of Dreams. When Tomoki looked up at the sky, it felt like they were inside of a dark dome. Thick clouds gathered in the dark sky, but here and there light would shine through. Sometimes a rainbow-colored membrane would appear, almost like an aurora in the sky. Above that were many bubbles that contained people's dreams. Each had a different form, and several different-sized dreams crowded around.

They would burst and then disappear. Some were dreams that had just been born. There were an infinite number of them, and sometimes they looked like they were glowing and overflowing.

"I'm pretty sure...it was a dream." Tomoki muttered to himself on the roof of the school building the next day. He and Yuugo had left during fourth period study hall and come up there. "Because I woke up in my own bed this morning." Tomoki had indeed woken up in his own room, in his own bed, that morning.

"I sent you there. You remember us going to the Depths of Dreams, right?"

"I dunno..." Tomoki didn't want to admit it, and held his head. "I can't remember!" He wanted to believe it was just a dream.

Yuugo gave up and shrugged. "You're a lot more stubborn than you look." He propped an elbow up on the fence and gazed out at the mountains in the distance. Clouds floated in the blue sky like white cotton. Underneath the dazzling sun, Tomoki couldn't help but think what happened in his dreams wasn't real. "Do you think I'm a liar?"

"That's not it," Tomoki said with a troubled look on his face.

Tomoki's life had been completely ordinary up until this point. There had been nothing extraordinary about it. He felt that was the best kind of life. "Are you telling me to believe that I'm someone like you, Yuugo? That I can be completely conscious even when I'm dreaming and think clearly and move freely? And fight demons and stuff? It just sounds like the hero of a science fiction movie or something."

"I'm not interested in heroes," Yuugo sighed. "I've been on the brink of death many times. I fought to survive. When we sleep, no matter what our intent, we fall to the Depths of Dreams. You should hurry and accept the truth and remember how to fight. There's no guarantee that I'll always be able to protect you."

"What do you mean, 'accept the truth?' I've had a normal life until now. I can't fight, and I don't have wings like you. I never wanna go to that creepy place again!"

"What are the names of the cat and the crow?"

"Jade and Kurou?" *Oh, crap!* Yuugo had asked him so casually that Tomoki had answered automatically.

"See, you remember! They're not attached emotionally to me, but to you!"

"But..." He just wanted to believe he had a weird dream the night before that Yuugo had wings and there was a talking cat and crow!

"Then let's fall again from a dark place in the school."

"No, I'm afraid to fall!"

Yuugo grabbed his arm, and Tomoki clung to the fence, his face pale. "Tomoki." He let go of Tomoki's arm and then held him close. His chestnut-colored hair smelled sweet, and turned a golden color in the sunlight. "Even though we've made love so many times, when we met at the school entrance ceremony, after that you'd never wake up in the Depths of Dreams. I guess it's because you didn't remember me at all in Reality." Tomoki became bright red at the soft sensation of Yuugo's hair brushing against his cheek. "You want so badly not to admit the truth, huh?"

"But...having sex...I'm a guy, you know," Tomoki said with tears in his eyes. It wasn't as if he didn't remember. But he had never even held hands with Yuugo in real life. He didn't think he was very feminine, and definitely didn't think Yuugo could think he was attractive. "Don't you have a girlfriend?"

"What are you talking about, all of a sudden?" Yuugo gaped. He felt dizzy. He had spent all this time trying to explain the circumstances to Tomoki, and he still didn't understand. "Will you get with it, already? You're my girlfriend!"

"What?!" Tomoki yelled out, his eyes wide.

"You're so thickheaded!"

"Well, you just said it so suddenly and..."

Yuugo sighed at the flustered Tomoki. "I don't think it was that sudden at all, but okay..." He had tried his best since the entrance ceremony to get Tomoki to remember him. "Well, I guess that part of you is pretty cute," Yuugo said shyly, scratching his head.

"Yuugo..." Tomoki whispered, still in disbelief.

Yuugo took his hands off the fence and held Tomoki in his arms. He looked at him and then pushed Tomoki down onto the floor of the roof. "Tomoki," Yuugo whispered into his ear.

Tomoki felt weak against the tenderness of Yuugo's voice and the sensual way he was staring at him. They leaned against the fence, Yuugo holding him. He lightly kissed Tomoki several times, searchingly. He licked Tomoki's lips with the tip of his tongue, and as Tomoki parted his lips to sigh, Yuugo thrust his moist tongue inside. "Mmm..." Tomoki sighed deeply. His pulse quickened, and his eyes became moist. Until then, he had only felt those kisses in his dreams. They lay down on the hard concrete, and he stroked Yuugo's back absentmindedly. "Yuugo..."

Between kisses, the bell rang. Tomoki's eyes snapped open, and he looked around wildly. He saw the blue sky over Yuugo's shoulder. He heard the noisy chatter of students below them just as the bell for lunch rang. "Ahhh!" Just as he came back to reality, Tomoki pushed Yuugo aside and sprang up. "What the hell was I doing?" He rushed to get down the stairs before the other kids who ate lunch on the roof came.

"No! I can't do this in Reality!" Tomoki smacked himself upside the head for letting himself get carried away. "Yuugo, we can't do this kind of thing at school!" Tomoki cautioned as they walked down the stairs.

"Yeah, I guess you're right. We won't be interrupted at my place."

"That's not what I mean! We can't do it anywhere people can see!" He pointed.

"So I can do anything I want in the Depths of Dreams?" Yuugo asked, and Tomoki was at a loss for words. He still couldn't admit what had happened in the dreams. "As long as it's not here in reality, it's okay, right?" Yuugo asked, raising the corners of his lips happily.

I wonder if I'll go there when I fall asleep tonight, Tomoki wondered during class that afternoon, propping his head on his hands. He had made Yuugo promise they wouldn't have sex in Reality, but he couldn't take responsibility for what happened in dreams. It wasn't like he could avoid going to sleep, and even though he kept it a secret from Yuugo, he was fully conscious and

remembered everything from his dreams.
That's why I trust myself even less...

"Where am I?" Tomoki looked around and blinked. He was still in his pajamas. A sweet fragrance drifted on the air in the white flower garden. The sky and the distant landscape was a pearl grey. There was no wind and the air seemed stagnant. Flower petals fell from the sky like snow.

"A safe place I found. It's someone else's dream, so it could disappear at any moment," Yuugo said. His black wings stood out against the white landscape. Tomoki was sitting on the soft flowers. He looked up at Yuugo, who was wearing a jean jacket, jeans, and high-top sneakers. His wings were a strange contrast to his normal-looking attire, and he seemed out of place in this unrealistic landscape.

"Those are pretty wings," Tomoki said innocently. The glossy black wings looked good on Yuugo, and made him look very heroic. "Can I touch them?" He pointed to them, and Yuugo smiled and nodded. He brought his wings a little closer, and Tomoki happily rubbed his cheek on them. They smelled like they had been out in the sun all day. He buried his face in their smoothness, and stroked them happily.

"Do you remember coming here, now?" Yuugo asked, smiling. Tomoki hugged his knees and shook his head. "I've been here a long time. As long as we don't fall in battle, we 'Dark Walkers' can live in this world."

"Dark Walkers?"

"That's what a samurai I met before called us. He had powers that allowed him to come to this world consciously, too." Yuugo folded up his wings and sat down next to Tomoki. "He was an old warrior from about four hundred years ago. He said it was the first time he had ever met one of his kind who had awoken so early." The samurai had saved Yuugo just as he was about to be eaten and carried him to a safe place. He had been bitten on his shoulder down to the bone, but in a few days his flesh had regenerated. In the Depths of Dreams, injuries healed much faster than they did in the world above.

"Your body won't get weak if you don't eat in this world. You'll never age and can continue living. The samurai said it was because of the nourishment in that water."

"It looks like an ocean, doesn't it? And there're all kinds of creatures that live really long in the ocean that haven't even been discovered yet. It's unbelievably big."

"That's right."

"And wounds will heal here, and your body doesn't age? It's like Heaven!"

"If you don't get eaten by demons." Yuugo smiled and nodded at Tomoki's cheerful outlook. But many kinds of demons also lived in this nourishing environment.

"Yuugo, did that samurai teach you how to fight against those demons?"

"Yeah. That's why my weapon of choice has always been a katana." The samurai was very skilled at swordsmanship and had defeated many demons. He had no ties to the world of reality, and wandered around this world like a pilgrim. Yuugo had been five years old when he had been saved by the samurai, and had become completely attached to the first "human" he had met. He had somehow become strong enough to defeat demons himself.

"It's a harsh existence. Monsters outnumber Dark Walkers," the samurai had said after seeing Yuugo's body bruised and beaten by battle. Everything Yuugo had learned about fighting, he had learned from that skilled warrior. The samurai had taught him how to draw his sword, and had even named it for him.

"Sleeping Tremor! Jade Thunder!" The name of the sword was frightening to demons.

Since then, like an incantation, Yuugo would speak its name and make his sword appear. When Yuugo became a competent fighter, the samurai wandered off on another journey without him. Yuugo didn't know if he was living somewhere in this world, or if he was dead. It seemed like this world had many strata that continued until Above Ground.

Even if a person with potential powers existed, there were very few among them who could enter the world of dreams with their bodies and consciousness intact. It was about the same probability of finding a jewel in the bottom of the ocean.

Sometimes they would see the faint silhouette of someone walking around. If they had come this far down, they probably had some powers, but they had no tangible body. If you touched one, your hand would go right through them, like an illusion. If you talked to them, they couldn't reply, and if demons gathered around and ate them, the worst that would happen to them would be that they woke up in Reality feeling sick.

It was much rarer to meet a "Dark Walker" who still had their flesh and blood intact.

"It's so strange," Tomoki whispered, hugging his knees to his chest. "You survived because of the samurai, and I survived because you saved me?"

"Yeah. I'm glad I found you," Yuugo answered in a serious voice. "After my relatives died, I didn't have any ties to the real world. I was here all by myself and thought I had no reason to be human anymore. I didn't know when I would turn into a demon ... But now that I have you, I can still be human."

"Yuugo..."

"Now that I have you, I can still be 'Yuugo Oda.'" Yuugo embraced Tomoki and kissed his head. He looked at Tomoki with tears in his eyes.

I'm the one who found him. Tomoki was finally fully conscious and with Yuugo. *He's finally mine...*

Almost a year earlier, in the Depths of Dreams that humans rarely went to, Tomoki had sat absentmindedly by himself, dreaming. Apparently he had fallen, still wearing his pajamas. He wasn't sure if that was the first time. He wasn't fully conscious, and there were all kinds of strange creatures around him. Tomoki stared at the demons almost as if they were butterflies dancing around the flower bed. The swarm of demons started licking him with their grotesquely long tongues.

They hadn't caught any game for a very long time, and decided that they'd violate Tomoki's flesh before eating it. Tomoki's white flesh was slippery with their saliva. He couldn't focus, and did not resist as the repulsive demons licked his erect desire, his hard nipples, his lips. He let out a small moan. Yuugo was stopped dead in his tracks by this immoral, obscene sight. Many hands spread both of Tomoki's legs apart, and the demons howled out in ecstasy. One giant demon with the head of a beast pushed his grotesque penis against Tomoki.

He's here in the flesh! Yuugo came back to himself as if he had just been punched in the face. If a sleeping human's consciousness hadn't substantiated there, there was no way that many demons would have been gathered around him. *He's a Dark Walker, like me. But how?!* He felt amazed and angry at the same time.

The demons were literally tearing the boy's body apart with their excited desires. They began to eat his flesh, stripping him down to the bone. There was no reason for them to let their trophy live. Yuugo took his sword that had materialized in one hand, spread his wings and flew into the demon's feast.

He slew them all, then stood panting on the mountain of their corpses. His body was drenched in blood, which drew a sharp desire in him to kill more. In the middle of this terrible scene, Tomoki stared up at him. His naked white body sat in the middle of the bloodbath, but his eyes were still peaceful and dreamy. He had almost been the demons' sacrificial lamb. Yuugo felt an intense hunger from the excitement of battle coupled with the memory of the boy's body being raped by the demons. *I fought to protect him...and I won. He belongs to me!*

Yuugo stretched out his arms and held the boy's warm body tightly against his chest. The boy stared up at Yuugo with wet, brown eyes. His skin was smooth and soft. Yuugo felt so much desire it almost made him go numb. When Yuugo pushed his hard rod into him, Tomoki gave a silent scream. He cried and shook his head in pain, but Yuugo couldn't be any gentler.

Yuugo held the boy's shoulders down tightly and buried his desire in Tomoki. His hips pumped hard. As if by instinct, Yuugo thrust deep inside him with one stroke. His throbbing need pressed hard against Tomoki's flesh. He was overcome by a dizzying sense of pleasure, and a beast-like scream came from his throat. Tomoki screamed and moaned in pain, but Yuugo couldn't hear it. It was like he had given in to carnal desire, like he was consuming the spoils of war. As he thrust his tongue deep into Tomoki's mouth, Yuugo pounded him harder. He didn't even realize it when Tomoki lost consciousness. He released his pleasure again and again inside Tomoki's warm body, which lay unmoving like a doll beneath him.

When Tomoki finally regained consciousness, he had looked up at Yuugo with red eyes. "It hurts," he had said in a hoarse voice. "It hurts!" Tears gathered in the corners of his eyes and then quickly traveled down his face. Yuugo was entranced by the beauty of it. Every time Tomoki's long eyelashes blinked, a large teardrop would fall. It was the first time Yuugo had ever seen someone his own age cry.

Before long, Tomoki had buried his face in his chest like a child who had been bullied.

"I'm sorry. I won't hurt you again, so stop crying. I'm sorry, it's all my fault," Yuugo apologized, not knowing what to do. "I'll be nice to you. I won't be mean again."

"You won't hurt me?" Tomoki asked, sniffling. The tip of his cute nose had turned bright red.

"No, I won't," Yuugo promised, stroking his hair. Tomoki seemed relieved and closed his eyes. His eyelids had trembled when Yuugo kissed his lips gently and held him. After Tomoki had disappeared from his arms, Yuugo figured he had either woken up or fallen into a normal sleep. *Next time, I'll ask him his name.* Yuugo smiled. He felt surprised at how natural the smile felt on his lips. He was content.

It was the first time he had touched someone else's skin, and he was so moved by it that his body still trembled. He had thought normal humans wouldn't understand a Dark Walker like himself. He had given up on ever living with or loving someone.

After his grandmother died, Yuugo hadn't been to Reality for over a year; he felt like Tomoki was the only person left in his whole world.

"Tomoki." He called out the name the boy had told him. He had come to see Yuugo every day, with the same earnest look in his eyes. When he made love to Tomoki, the wild excitement from battle was calmed. Sometimes Tomoki accepted him in his arms like a lover searching

for another body. The feeling of his gasping body in his arms was so precious. Yuugo had protected him now for almost a whole year...

You don't want to?" Yuugo asked, sighing. Tomoki was sitting in his lap, still wearing his pajamas. When Yuugo tried to kiss him, Tomoki had unconsciously pulled away.

"But...you promised you wouldn't have sex with me," Tomoki said, turning red. He was definitely fully conscious. His body was real, down to the way he breathed and the way his skin smelled faintly of sweat.

"You're dreaming right now."

"I know, but..." Tomoki got goosebumps from the way Yuugo whispered into his ear. His voice was familiar, as was his heartbeat and the way he breathed. Tomoki felt his eyes getting moist, as he remembered "his" body from his dreams.

"If it's a dream, it's okay, right?" Yuugo kissed him, and Tomoki felt the core of his body starting to grow warm. He didn't want to admit it, but his body was responding to Yuugo.

This...is a dream, Tomoki whispered as an excuse when the last of his reason had disappeared.

"Ah...Yuugo..." He moaned as Yuugo playfully bit his earlobe.

Towards the end of May, Tomoki had started going to Yuugo's condo often. Today was Friday, and starting tomorrow they had two days off from school. After parting with Yuugo at the park, he hurried home and changed. Tomoki brought his overnight bag and started to leave the house. His mother had given him some snacks, which made him happy.

Since the first time Yuugo had eaten dinner at their house, Tomoki's mother had become a huge fan of his smile. When she heard he lived alone, she gave Yuugo some leftovers in a plastic container.

Tomoki entered the pass code Yuugo had given him at the entrance of the building, then stepped inside. He had the spare key in his pocket. "I'm here!"

"Hey," Yuugo called as Tomoki came inside. He was wearing jeans and a T-shirt and was in the middle of assembling some furniture in the living room. He had even bought some power tools for the job. Tomoki put the plastic container in the fridge and started to wash some rice. They had bought a rice cooker the other day. Tomoki had asked his mother how to wash and prepare rice so he could show Yuugo. It almost felt like they were at camp. It was fun to populate the empty room with various things.

"Yuugo, the sofa's here, so let's carry it over there." A young delivery man had brought the sofa, and they carried it into the living room. It was upholstered in soft, grey fabric, and was long enough to lie down on. Several more deliveries came, and they began discussing where each appliance or piece of furniture should go. There was a rug and a dining table for two. They set up the entertainment center in the corner and hooked up the TV and stereo.

They had gone shopping for the simple furniture together, but Yuugo didn't have any preferences so Tomoki had ended up picking out most of them. They made the largest room near the foyer the bedroom and moved the bed in there, and then concentrated on furnishing the living room. They had chosen high quality furniture, so it hadn't been cheap, but Tomoki hadn't used even half of the budget Yuugo had given him. It had turned into the ideal apartment. A potted plant next to the sofa would complete the look, but instead they went with a floor lamp. As Tomoki checked his notebook, he confirmed what deliveries would be coming that day. *When Yuugo finishes assembling the computer desk, that should be the last one.*

"It looks good, doesn't it?"

"Do you like it?"

"Yeah." Yuugo was impressed as he looked around the finished room. Even though it was mostly decorated in grey, the room seemed warm. In the dining area there was the table and computer desk. A grey rug was spread out in the living room and the sofa was against the window. The TV was on the entertainment center across from it in the corner.

"Well, let's eat dinner." Tomoki was happy that Yuugo looked happy.

"Rice is a lot better than convenience store food."

Even though Tomoki's mother usually did the cleaning, he had fun tidying up the brand new kitchen. After dinner he made some coffee, and set two cups on the table in front of the sofa. As they both sat on the sofa drinking coffee, they watched TV.

"You can really relax when you have a sofa, huh?" Tomoki said.

"Yeah, our living room at home was just *tatami* so I never had one."

"What was your house like, Yuugo? Did you eat Japanese food all the time?"

"Yeah. The servants never fixed Western food. For desert it was always fruit or sweet bean jelly. The first time I went to a convenience store, I tried all kinds of stuff."

Many food commercials came on in between shows, and as they watched them they talked about the various things they liked. "Oh, those are so good!"

"Yeah, I like those, too...Is this what normal life is like?" Yuugo asked as he stretched out on the couch.

"Yep. Hey, what kind of person was your grandma? Did she know about your powers or about the Depths of Dreams?" Tomoki asked curiously.

Yuugo brushed his hair from his face. "It's not that interesting."

"But I want to know more about you," Tomoki said seriously.

"Grandma called the Depths of Dreams 'Hell.' She pitied those who could go there with their bodies intact. My dad was a Dark Walker, too."

"Your dad was, too?"

Yuugo spoke softly as they listened to the laughter on the television. "One day his body disappeared from reality. If you get hurt in the dream world, your real body is hurt, too. I heard that sometimes he came back bleeding and had to be taken to the hospital. If you get eaten in the Depths of Dreams, your dead body doesn't return to Reality, just like my dad's."

"Did your mom know about this?"

"Mom thought it was just a regular missing person case. She was a very realistic woman." Yuugo sighed and propped his head against the back of the couch. When he had first fallen into the Depths of Dreams, he had been afraid that his body would disappear and clung to his mother. *"Mom, save me!"* But his mother had looked at him in horror and screamed. She pried his hands loose like she was trying to shake off something disgusting. Yuugo could never forget the look of fear on his mother's face.

Her child had fallen into the underworld, still trying to clutch at her hands. He wanted to think her fear was instinctual, that she had been afraid he might drag her down, too. *"Mom, I'm scared! Mooomm!!"* He had kept calling out as he cried. Her back was pressed up against the wall, her hands over her ears. She kept shaking her head back and forth as if she were crazy. Ever since then, she would look at Yuugo with frightened eyes when he came back. Even if he was bleeding, she would act like she didn't notice. When he'd reach out his arms to her, she'd scream and smack his hands away.

So Yuugo didn't tell his mother anything about it. He was terrified of falling into the Depths of Dreams. He started to dislike his mother, who rarely even talked to him. "So after that, my mom remarried and brought me to my dad's mother's house. I'm sure she didn't want to live with a kid who disappeared and reappeared all the time. But my grandmother accepted me. She knew her own child, my dad, had also 'fallen' before."

So that's why his grandma was so nice to him.

Before Yuugo's grandmother died, she had apologized to him for not sending him to school and limiting his contact with the outside world. She had told him she did it so others wouldn't learn about his special abilities. She told him with tears in her eyes, "From now on, you'll meet lots of people. Just keep a smile on your face. Humans won't dislike or doubt those that always smile."

After she died, Yuugo felt there was no worth to Reality anymore. He didn't have anyone he loved. Even though he had property and an inheritance, he didn't know anything about the outside world and had no interest in them. Until he met Tomoki, Yuugo really thought he would give up on Reality for good. He never thought he would be as happy as he was now.

"So I guess I've had a bit of bad luck."

"Not just a bit!" Tomoki said sorrowfully, with his fists clenched. "I can't believe how cruel your mother is! It's not like it was your fault! It's not your fault you fell into the dream world!" He wiped the tears from his face.

"My mom is like a stranger to me now, so it's not a big deal."

Tomoki held Yuugo's strong body to his chest. "Your mom should have held you like this when you were little..." If one of Yuugo's parents had been able to understand him, he wouldn't have been so scared. Tomoki wished he could have been there for him.

"Tomoki." Yuugo smiled and softly touched

Tomoki's hair. He rubbed his warm cheek against Tomoki's wet one. With their warm bodies against each other, it made him remember painful memories of the past even more.

Tomoki had had a happy childhood, so that's why he had so much love and could be so kind. His smiles were genuine, unlike Yuugo's. Before they realized it, it had gotten so late that the credits rolled on the TV show they had been watching and the channel was signing off for the night. White noise filled the room.

"Tomoki," Yuugo said quietly after a while. He turned the TV off with the remote control and looked at Tomoki, who had his face buried in Yuugo's chest.

"Hmm?" Tomoki's face went bright red as Yuugo pulled him closer. Tomoki had been holding him to comfort him a little while ago, but at some point, Yuugo had become the one holding him. Tomoki had gotten so comfortable and relaxed with Yuugo stroking his back and his hair that he had dozed off. "I'm sorry, I..." He looked up at the clock and saw it had been almost two hours.

"It's okay. You're cute when you're asleep," Yuugo said, smiling. A cheerful expression replaced the depressed one he had worn a while ago. "If you're gonna sleep, let's go to bed."

"Okay," he answered cheerfully, and then remembered something important. There was only one bed.

"It's a double bed, so it should be okay, right?" Yuugo said, sensing Tomoki's worry.

"Are you sure it's okay?"

"It's big, don't worry about it." Yuugo nodded exaggeratedly.

Tomoki said silently, *"It's you I'm worried about, not the bed!"*

He took a shower and then changed into his pajamas. Yuugo watched him as he dried his hair in front of the bathroom mirror with a blow-dryer. "Yuugo?" Tomoki motioned him closer. "This is how you use this." He leaned over and ran his fingers through Yuugo's half-dried hair, blowing the warm air from the blow-dryer on it.

"I can tell from watching you!" Yuugo chuckled. "I'm not *that* stupid!" They both smiled at the same time.

"Things are gonna get rough from now on," Yuugo said as they lie in bed, looking up at the ceiling. The light from the lamp tinted the room a light orange.

"I know," Tomoki nodded as he held onto the edge of the bed. "You saved me when I was in a dangerous place, right?"

"Yeah." Yuugo's low voice echoed in the quiet room.

"Hey," Tomoki turned towards Yuugo and said timidly. "I don't remember it, but thanks."

"Huh?" Yuugo brought his face closer, as if he hadn't heard Tomoki.

"I'm probably still alive because of you. I just wanted to thank you," Tomoki explained, smiling. "I'm not one hundred percent convinced yet, but it looks like I go there every day whether I know it or not."

"Yeah. It would be best if you'd awaken soon."

Yuugo held Tomoki close to him, but Tomoki tried to push him away.

"Y-You promised we wouldn't have sex in real life!"

Yuugo sighed exasperatedly.

"You drive me crazy..."

If he had accepted everything else, what was the difference if they did it in Reality or in dreams? When Yuugo forcibly held Tomoki and pressed his lips upon him, Tomoki would look down. When Yuugo tried to tilt his chin upwards, Tomoki would bury his face in the sheets.

"I don't remember being lovers with you for a whole year, yet," his muffled voice said.

"Your body remembers," Yuugo leaned over and whispered into his ear. Tomoki started to tremble. He felt his body start to grow hot and sweaty.

"I said no! If you're gonna force me, I'm going home!" Tomoki yelled as Yuugo tried to unbutton his pants.

"Then just let me kiss you."

"No! If you do, I'll go home!" Tomoki clutched the sheets, like a cat clawing desperately at a wall.

"Fine, I won't do anything."

"I'm sorry."

"Don't apologize!" Yuugo said in an irritated voice and sighed. "You just won't be honest with yourself!" He scratched his head and left for the bathroom.

Tomoki's grip on the sheets relaxed, and he sighed. He hadn't had sex with another man in Reality yet. That was his last reason to resist. But he could feel his body responding to Yuugo's touch. If he didn't have strong willpower, he would let Yuugo have his way. Since the line between dreams and reality was vague, he didn't want Yuugo to think he could do whatever he wanted with him.

Tomoki wasn't sure how he felt inside. He didn't know if he loved Yuugo because they had sex in their dreams, or if they had sex because he loved him. He couldn't remember that important thing.

Now that Tomoki was able to dream consciously, he realized something important. After he fell into the Depths of Dreams after their last conversation, Yuugo was still angry.

"Yuugo!" he yelled, running from here to there, trying to escape the vulgar demons.

"Aren't you gonna save him?" Jade asked as she pawed at Yuugo's back. He was dressed in his usual comfortable jean jacket and jeans, lying on top of a mountain.

"It's not my fault if he won't face the truth. He won't die because of those weaklings, anyway."

"You're the one who can't face the truth!" Jade pushed a paw against Yuugo's cheek. He was being so childish.

"Yuugo, you bastard!" Tomoki was running around desperately, and a slimy, sticky thing came at him from the darkness. The dirty brown monster stuck to Tomoki's arm and spread out its body, like an octopus spreading out its tentacles. "Ahhh! I'm gonna be eaten!"

He screamed at the disgusting feeling on his skin. It felt like raw rubber. Just as he grabbed it, a green flame burst from his fist, causing the sticky monster to burst into flames. He quickly shook his hand, and the cold flame fell to the ground along with the slime.

"Huh?" He looked at his hand and saw a golden-green flame. When he squeezed his hand and then opened it, it glowed brighter and then disappeared. When he began to walk again, the other monsters seemed frightened and backed away.

"Looks like he remembered 'Flame Fist.'"

"Lord Tomoki is so strong!" Jade and Kurou were impressed.

"Now if only he can make his weapon appear, he'd be complete," Yuugo whispered as he gazed at the dark sky. In this world, the power of one's spirit was everything. If you focused, the human body could be very strong. Taking on a fighting stance, pumping your fist and yelling, "Get away!" could be very effective against monsters, even if you didn't know what you were doing. Even silently willing something to "Disappear!" or "Burst into flames!" could be a very effective offensive and defensive tactic.

But the only sure thing was to have a reliable weapon like Yuugo's. If you trained with it diligently, the sword would become sharp and strong. And it was best to give the sword a name. If its master called for it by name, it would materialize in his hands instantly.

"Do you want me to save you?" Yuugo said in a carefree voice to Tomoki, who had been running from demons and monsters like a chicken with its head cut off.

"You're such a bully!" Tomoki said, panting.

"It's just a dream, so it's okay, right?" Yuugo used his own words against him. Tomoki groaned and then grew pale. He realized he had just been afraid that if he died in his dreams, he'd die in real life.

Yuugo crossed his arms behind his head and smiled. "This is pretty funny." He looked satisfied. Before, like the "Sleeping Beauty" Tomoki had mentioned, he had closed his eyes and rejected him time and time again. Yuugo had thought he was just a quiet pretty boy—but now that he saw him angry, Yuugo decided that this side of Tomoki was much more lively and interesting. It made him seem even more attractive than before.

"Yuugo!" He jumped up, hearing Tomoki's screams. "Help me!" Tomoki was running towards him, his face pale. A demon that resembled a dragon was crawling from the darkness. It was creeping along like a snake. It was unbelievably large, probably taller than a two-story building. It gazed at Tomoki with a pair of glowing, red eyes. *No monster like this exists in Reality!*

It opened its mouth wide, revealing sharp fangs. It looked hungry.

"Tomoki, take cover as fast as you can!" Yuugo ran and jumped over Tomoki's head from behind. "Jade Thunder!" Just as he called its name, a glittering sword appeared. He sliced the sharp blade into the dragon's neck. It didn't seem to realize what had just happened and froze momentarily. Only when it turned its head did it give a deep, guttural cry. The cut had been so fine even the defeated dragon hadn't realized it at first. As he stared at the dragon's neck that lay wriggling at his feet, Yuugo shook his sword. The dark liquid on it turned into dark red smoke and then vanished.

"Are you okay, Tomoki?"

"Yeah, I'm fine." Yuugo turned around and saw Tomoki far away, waving to him. "Ahh, that scared me! I didn't think something that big was here!" Tomoki smiled and started to walk towards him when suddenly the hair on the back of Yuugo's neck stood on end.

"Tomoki!" he screamed as he saw some kind of black tentacle reach behind Tomoki in the darkness.

"Ahhh!" Tomoki's face contorted with pain and he clutched at the black thing that coiled around his body. Goosebumps spread all over him. The dragon's tongue wriggled inside his fist disgustingly, and he immediately let go of it, as if he had been electrocuted. "Yuugo!" he screamed, reaching his arms out towards him. Suddenly the ground was far away, and his legs were kicking in mid air. He must have been very high up, because Yuugo's figure got smaller and smaller on the ground. The dragon's reptilian eyes stared at him in the darkness. It opened its large mouth wide, revealing rows of sharp fangs. Its breath was warm and smelled of something raw. Tomoki started to feel faint.

"Oohhh, Lord Tomoki is in trouble!" Kurou shouted excitedly, flapping around Yuugo.

"Yuugo, you can't! That one's too strong! If you fight him, you'll turn into a real demon!"

"But if he does not save him, Lord Tomoki will be eaten!"

"But, but, but, Yuugoooo!"

Not paying any attention to their quarrel, Yuugo stared at the dragon's eyes. Deep in the darkness, he could see other giant figures crawling around. A cold sweat spread over his forehead, and he sighed.

"Yuugo!" Jade cried shrilly. She knew they couldn't get to him now. His eyes were filled with the desire to kill. Her fur stood up on end. Yuugo kicked off the ground, and spread his wings with a loud flapping noise. "Yuugo!" Jade clawed the ground to keep herself steady against the strong wind.

With just a few flaps of his wings, Yuugo had disappeared into the darkness.

"Yuugo went to fight."

"I should have stopped him," Jade said with tears in her eyes.

"What should we do now?" Kurou asked, flapping around.

"Escape so we don't get in the middle of it!"

"Got it!" The golden cat and the crow bounded away, leaving the battlefield behind them.

"Sleeping Tremor..." Yuugo kicked off the ground and flapped his wings. "Come to me, Jade Thunder!" He called the weapon back to his hands. Two black lines appeared on his face with a flash. Since he had absorbed the powers of a certain demon he had defeated, they always appeared before battle. They almost looked like tiger stripes, or war paint. Leather gloves appeared on his hands, and dull silver arm and leg guards materialized.

"Tomoki!" He sliced at the air as he watched Tomoki about to be taken into the dragon's mouth. Suddenly he shoved his blade into one of the dragon's eyes.

"Gyaaaaaa!" The dragon shook its head and opened its mouth wide in pain. Its tongue was still wrapped around Tomoki, who tried to twist out of its grip. Just as he was on the verge of being pierced by one of the dragon's sharp fangs, Yuugo swung his sword onto its tongue. The dismembered tongue squirmed, squeezing Tomoki, who had fallen unconscious. Yuugo wrestled him free from the smelly tongue, but just when he had let his guard down another dragon attacked him from the side. Yuugo barely dodged it, and could hear the clicking sound of the dragon's fangs.

Dozens of pairs of eyes stared at Yuugo from the darkness. "Shit!" he screamed. He held the unconscious Tomoki in one arm, so he couldn't move quickly or use his sword. He returned to the ground again and softly laid Tomoki's body down in the shadow of a mountain.

I guess I have to fight them...

He looked at Tomoki, whose eyes were closed, and gulped hard. Even though he was fast, it would be impossible to fly away carrying him. There were numerous dragons high in the sky with tongues as fierce as whips. He didn't know what would happen to him if he fought such large demons, but he knew he couldn't let Tomoki be eaten.

He turned back to look at Tomoki once more and then narrowed his eyes. He gripped his katana in both hands and leaned forward. His enemies had tongues like whips and long necks. They had fangs and sharp, reptilian claws on their feet that glittered black. When he got the chance, Yuugo kicked off the ground and flew into the group of red eyes.

The blade of his katana blocked their sharp claws with a *clang*, and he dodged them with a yell. He slew all the dragons blocking his way and was drenched in the blood that gushed from their bodies. The katana that had protected him since he was five was sharp and gleamed even before these formidable enemies.

If he let his guard down for even a moment, a sharp, steel-like claw would come slicing towards him. Yuugo cut the dragons in two with his sword. His adrenaline pumped, and he got so excited he almost forgot what his objective was. When he focused his energy like this, his muscles became as strong as a beast's. He forgot human emotions like fear or cowardice. His body trembled with pleasure from his slaughter, and for a while he was lost in it. His katana had become his own fangs, his own claws that he was free to manipulate.

"Yuugo....," Tomoki said in a trembling voice after he had regained consciousness. All he could do was watch, dumbfounded, as the heroic scene unfolded around him.

Yuugo slew every dragon that faced him, one after another. His jet black wings and his body were soaked in blood; he almost looked like a demon from Hell. After he had defeated all of his enemies, Yuugo stood in the center of the ruins. He had been wounded in battle, and blood ran down his leg.

"Yuugo..."

Tomoki rushed over to him, his face pale.

"Tomoki," Yuugo whispered. He shook the blood off his katana, which disappeared into the air after its duty had been finished. Yuugo still panted. Tomoki wanted to smile to comfort him, but his face looked so distorted.

"Yuugo?" Tomoki reached out both hands worriedly, and Yuugo fell to his knees. His whole body began to strangely convulse.

"Guuaahhh!" A beast-like roar came from the back of his throat. His left arm flailed, clawing at the air, and he grabbed it with his other arm, trying to hold it down. Cold sweat ran down his face from fear and intense pain. He gritted his teeth against the unbearable pain.

"Yuugo..." The color drained from Tomoki's face. A single large, black claw had just sprouted from Yuugo's left elbow, tearing through his skin. Then, the same kind of demon claws ripped out of his fingers. His body had started to transform into a demon's. It seemed that Yuugo had absorbed the powers and characteristics of the demons he had just defeated.

"Tomoki...Tomoki, save me!" he cried. The one who was most scared at that moment wasn't Tomoki, but Yuugo. "Tomoki..." His flesh burned, and he felt faint from the pain in his left arm. It exceeded fear. Even though he was writhing against the pain, it was as if he was being controlled by an evil demon. It felt like his instincts for fighting and killing and feeding were going wild. In the back of his mind, Yuugo thought he was done for.

I can't be human anymore...I'm a demon

now...When I wake up, the human known as Yuugo Oda will be gone...

All he'd be able to do is remain in that world, an ugly demon.

"No! No!" The sight of Tomoki was his only relief, and it started to sway. "No! Don't go, Tomoki!" He didn't know why he was crying so desperately.

"Yuugo, snap out of it! Yuugo!" Tomoki called his name and held onto Yuugo's trembling body. "I'm right here, Yuugo. I'm holding you!"

"Tomoki, Tomoki..."

"It's okay, Yuugo. I'm holding you. Don't worry."

Yuugo sobbed and held onto Tomoki frantically. His claws dug into Tomoki's back.

"I'm right here," Tomoki held Yuugo's body against his. Tomoki called Yuugo's name many times, trying to soothe him, but he still cried out in pain. His bloody body continued to change. He had slaughtered so many demons with his sword.

Tomoki had just seen him fight for the first time, and remembered how scared it had made him. He almost thought that the Yuugo he knew had been an impersonator. But now, as he turned into a demon, Yuugo seemed so scared.

"I remember, now," Tomoki said tearfully as he pushed his cheek against Yuugo's, who was still howling in pain. "I remember everything about you, now." He smiled gently and kissed Yuugo's lips.

Tomoki remembered everything from his first encounter with Yuugo. Yuugo had defeated a demon who had tried to eat Tomoki, and he had been drenched

in blood just like he was now. *I remember.* They had made love so many times, sometimes maddeningly roughly, sometimes sweetly and gently.

"This time, I'm going to save you." Tomoki took Yuugo's arms and held Yuugo's precious body close against him.

"Yuugo, does it still hurt?" Tomoki looked up worriedly. He sat on the floor while Yuugo sat on his bed. He had bandaged up his arm until it turned back into a "human" arm. "Are you okay? Have you calmed down?"

"Yeah," Yuugo answered, looking down. Tomoki sat next to him on the bed. Yuugo stared down at the hand that had just had claws growing from it and sighed. He pushed back his hair. The feeling of his fingers was back, and Yuugo sighed again with a painful look on his face. "Are you scared that my body changed?"

"No." Tomoki rubbed his red eyes and shook his head. Sitting on the bed, he took Yuugo's hand between his. He remembered what had happened before. Yuugo had screamed in pain and cried, and Tomoki had held him.

Why wasn't Tomoki scared after such a terrible thing had happened? When Yuugo had held onto him, it was as if he was clinging onto him, searching for warmth. He was clinging to anything that was human. He was desperately clinging to his desire to be loved by someone.

That's how much both Yuugo's body and heart had been wounded. Even though Tomoki hadn't been fully conscious, he had understood Yuugo's heart clearly. That's why he had been able to accept him. He was sure Yuugo had kissed him so gently afterwards to try to calm him, so he wouldn't cry. He had held Yuugo and stroked his hair.

"Tomoki, I might turn into a demon," Yuugo reached a hand up to gently touch Tomoki's cheek.

"No, you won't." Tomoki smiled, his pretty amber eyes crinkling, and put his own hand on Yuugo's. It was the hand that had had claws coming from it. Yuugo had thought Tomoki would be scared and would pull away from his embrace. He hadn't realized he had clung to Tomoki's back so hard that his claws had dug into it. They weren't bleeding anymore, but the cuts that were visible through Tomoki's ripped pajamas looked painful.

"I might hurt you more, Tomoki. I might lose control and eat you," Yuugo whispered painfully.

"It doesn't hurt anymore. And if it looks like you'll turn into a demon, I'll heal you—so don't worry." He hugged Yuugo, trying to cheer him up. Actually, Tomoki had no idea whether or not he even had those powers, but he wanted to do anything to soothe Yuugo. "You're so handsome, it would be a shame if you weren't human anymore."

"Tomoki." Yuugo smiled, but then covered his face with his hands. Tomoki's kindness had helped lift the uneasy feeling he had in the pit of his stomach. His body felt warm. Warm in a way he had never known until he met Tomoki.

He felt better just being with him. He felt like it

was because of Tomoki that he was still human. He was the only one who could save Yuugo from his wildness. Still covering his face, he gulped. "I...want you to stay with me. I love you," Yuugo said in a choked voice.

Tomoki blushed slightly at Yuugo's confession. "I know." His throat felt tight, and that was all he could say. He had wanted to hear those words so much. Yuugo hadn't even said them in his dreams when they made love. He wanted Tomoki so much and had treasured him so much, but he hadn't said those words until now. "I would have felt a lot better if you'd have said that earlier." When he thought of when they first met, he suddenly understood. Maybe at first, it had been pity. He wanted to make love to Yuugo because he felt his uncertainty and fear. No matter what bad things had happened in his life, he had always unconsciously searched for him in the depths of his dreams. He wanted to accept all of him. Because he loved him.

He finally understood how he felt. "I love you, too, Yuugo," he said honestly, his voice hoarse. "You're so stupid, though," he whispered bitterly, and, after he closed his eyes, tears dripped onto his lap. "If you had just told me from the beginning, I would have been yours even then..." Tomoki looked up and smiled, his eyes full of tears. He was so happy his chest was trembling, but his face was hot and he couldn't stop crying.

"Tomoki." At just the sound of Yuugo calling his name, Tomoki's body went weak. Yuugo tilted his chin up and kissed Tomoki's hot face. He looked at him with love in his eyes. Their tongues intertwined until they grew numb. Yuugo held Tomoki gently in his arms. He showed his true face to Tomoki when he smiled at him now. Those eyes that were so full of love were only for Tomoki.

"Yuugo..." Tomoki's voice was muffled by kisses. Yuugo's tongue traced his lips, making him moan. His wet tongue slid inside his mouth. He licked around inside, making the hair stand up on the back of Tomoki's neck.

They lay down on the bed, still kissing, and he moaned from the feeling of Yuugo's body on top of him. "Mmm..." Yuugo's smooth tongue teased him. They had kissed many times in the Depths of Dreams, but his heart was pounding so fast he felt like it would explode. Yuugo bit his earlobe playfully, and Tomoki's face grew hot with embarrassment.

Yuugo unbuttoned Tomoki's pajamas, and traced his fingers along Tomoki's bare skin. Yuugo found his erect nipples and teased them with his fingertips.

"Yuugo..."

He licked all the way up to Tomoki's neck, making his lips tremble. They stripped off all their clothes, and Tomoki lay face down on the bed, Yuugo holding him. The weight of his body was painful, but the sensation of his smooth skin was so pleasant Tomoki felt like he would melt. Even though he wanted to turn off the lights, no matter how much he squirmed he couldn't resist the fingers that moved beneath him. Yuugo knew Tomoki was hard, but purposefully stroked his inner thigh slowly.

He kissed Tomoki's soft brown hair and the nape of his neck, and Tomoki's pale skin flushed a light pink. Yuugo searched for his erogenous zones as his fingers traveled downward until he touched Tomoki's hardness. Tomoki's moans became more frequent, more sensual. His eyes became wet. He felt Yuugo's hard member pushing against his back, and then raised his hips naturally.

"Ahhhh!" Yuugo teased him with his tongue and fingers and, just as he had in Tomoki's dreams, coaxed a moan of pleasure from his lips.

"Tomoki," Yuugo sighed into his ear, holding him from behind. Tomoki trembled from the way Yuugo's long fingers stroked him, and his desire swelled even more. He felt Yuugo's breath upon his neck, and his hard head pushing between Tomoki's legs.

"Aahhh!" Tomoki cried out in a painful voice as Yuugo's overwhelming manhood pierced through his soft flesh. Yuugo buried his hardness to its base, deep within Tomoki, and Tomoki clutched the sheets as he arched his back. He felt dizzy, and when Yuugo withdrew and then plunged himself back in again, Tomoki let out another yell.

"Yuugo..." he whispered. He felt like Yuugo was squeezing every drop of pleasure from him. Yuugo flipped his sensitive body over and placed both Tomoki's legs over his shoulders. He leaned down and kissed Tomoki, who eagerly kissed back. Both their bodies were hot, and their sweat and rough breathing mixed together. Yuugo's hardness plunged in again, and Tomoki's body shook as if he were in the middle of a stormy sea. "Yuugo..." He clung to Yuugo's strong back as if that would keep him from being carried away.

That night, Tomoki sat on Yuugo's bed, watching as he went to turn off the lights. He was going to try to fall into the Depths of Dreams while fully conscious. Even if there was just a little darkness, they could move to another type of darkness, in dreams. That's why they were called "Dark Walkers."

Tomoki was wearing a white cotton shirt, jeans and sneakers. "Remember what you're wearing right now," Yuugo said, pointing to his clothes. He sat on the edge of the bed in bare feet, also wearing a cotton shirt and jeans. "Open your eyes and remember how your clothes feel on you." He lifted Tomoki up and placed him in his lap. The room was dark. Once his eyes had adjusted to the darkness, Tomoki looked at Yuugo with an uneasy look on his face.

"It's okay. I'm right here," Yuugo said, and gave him a soft kiss. "Once the floor and bed disappear, just pretend like you're diving in the ocean."

"The ocean?"

"Just imagine it. You were scared before when there was nothing beneath your feet, right? So let's fall slowly," he explained kindly.

So when I had that sense of vertigo last time, it was just an illusion? Tomoki thought as he nodded against Yuugo's chest. Ever since they had become lovers, Yuugo had been extremely kind to Tomoki in his dreams and Reality. So much so that it had almost become a problem at school.

"Are you ready? Here we go."

"Okay." Tomoki gulped and held onto Yuugo. Even though they were together, his heart pounded violently.

Yuugo had told him to imagine the ocean, but all Tomoki could do was stare at the digital clock on the other side of the room that read "9:13."

Suddenly the numbers seemed to be floating in mid-air. Tomoki looked up in surprise, and, at that moment, realized they were falling through the floor. Yuugo's condo was on the ninth floor, and even though there should have been someone else's room below them, there was nothing below Tomoki's feet.

They had moved from Reality to dreams.

"You don't have to hold me so tightly. You won't fall," Yuugo said, and Tomoki loosened his grip. He felt relieved at the gentle smile on Yuugo's face. They were falling into the dark space slowly, and it almost felt as if they were swimming through a warm liquid. His body felt lighter than it did in reality. When he thought about sinking further, he'd sink further, and he felt like he could float in midair if he wanted to. His body didn't feel hot or cold. When he breathed in, the air felt moist, like just before a typhoon.

"You're always in your pajamas, huh?" When they both reached the ground, Yuugo laughed as he put Tomoki down.

"Ah, you're right!"

"You're not wearing any shoes, either," he said, pointing to Tomoki's bare feet. He, on the other hand, was wearing his normal sneakers.

"I wonder why I took them off?"

"It's because you think this is a dream, so you end up in your pajamas and bare feet. If you just imagine it, you can wear the clothes and shoes you just had on. And sometimes, if you're not careful, you can end up going back to Reality naked!"

"So it wouldn't be good if you were barefoot?"

"I'm going back to my room, so it's okay."

"But when we came here before, I was in my school uniform, and then I was in my pajamas," Tomoki whispered, confused. And when he had woken up the next morning, he was in his own bed with his pajamas on and his school uniform was hanging up in the closet as usual. That's why he had thought it had been a dream.

"I brought you back to your room and changed you."

"You can come into my room? Have you come before while I was asleep?" Tomoki was shocked.

"All I did was drop you off so you wouldn't get lost."

"Hey. Once I saw a silhouette in my room that had wings. Was that you? I thought something strange had come in."

"Hey, I'm not that persistent!" Yuugo said indignantly. "Why would I have to go into your room, anyway? We always have sex in our dreams. I only brought you back because there were so many demons around your house back then, so it was dangerous."

"Seriously? But I thought demons can't come into Reality."

"That's what I thought, too. But even I don't know everything about this world. If one of them was really in your room..."

"I'm sorry, I believe you." He felt bad when he saw

the serious look on Yuugo's face. "I'm sorry." He held onto Yuugo's arm and apologized again.

"Okay. First, imagine your clothes." Tomoki touched his pajamas. He felt the buttons and the softness of the fabric. But he had been wearing a white cotton T-shirt before they had fallen. It was fairly new, so he couldn't remember its design clearly.

"You really love that jean jacket, don't you?" Tomoki couldn't picture his clothes clearly, so he opened his eyes and stared at Yuugo's clothes. With his jet-black wings, they made him look tough. He unbuttoned Yuugo's shirt and stroked his chest as he looked on and smiled. The feeling of the soft fabric and his soft skin was exactly the same as in real life.

Even though he had been barefoot before, he had on his favorite basketball shoes. When Tomoki leaned over, he saw that even the shoelaces were untied, and the soles of his shoes were rubber.

"Just think of some clothes you remember well."

"Wow!" When he pulled on Yuugo's jeans, he was impressed that he was even wearing underwear. "There's even a tag on them!" The brand-name tag was still on Yuugo's favorite pair of boxers.

"Don't worry about the tag. The only reason it's there is because I remembered it well," Yuugo said, laughing as he saw the worried look on Tomoki's face.

"Does this look weird?" Tomoki turned around, and Yuugo gave him the "okay" sign.

"So you settled on your school uniform after all, huh?"

"I can't remember any of my other clothes as well," Tomoki said indignantly as Yuugo laughed at him. Since he wore his familiar school uniform every day, it was the easiest thing to imagine.

"It's okay. Much better than pajamas."

"I'll work on wearing regular shoes, too."

"Clothes aren't important. Concentrate on armor to protect yourself. Leather is good to start with. Concentrate and focus on the feel of the material, the weight of it."

"So it's like magic?"

"Yes. You can make anything appear here as long as you can picture it and believe you can."

"Leather armor..." Tomoki whispered and closed his eyes in concentration. He tried to imagine the smell of leather and the feel of it, and then felt the tangible sensation of leather in his hands. He felt the weight of it, and grasped it with both hands before it could disappear.

"You think you can protect yourself with that?" Yuugo sighed.

"Huh?" In Tomoki's hands was his familiar leather school bag. The leather bag definitely wouldn't provide any defense against demons. "I guess I always conjure up things I remember the best." He opened the bag and searched inside. Even his pencils, textbooks, notebooks and his wallet were inside. "Oh, shit!" he exclaimed. Yuugo looked at him curiously.

"I forgot to do my math homework!" Tomoki said seriously as he looked through his notebook, and Yuugo sat down on the floor.

"Tomoki, your school bag is all wrong. Stop getting distracted by your homework and start thinking about the enemy!" Yuugo said, pointing at him.

"Oooh, Lord Tomoki is safe!" Kurou came flying from the other side of the darkness.

"I'm so glad Yuugo wasn't turned into a demon!" Jade said happily.

"I was so worried about Lord Tomoki I could not sleep last night!"

"You don't even have to sleep!"

"I love the human Yuugo!" Jade jumped on Yuugo's shoulder, purred and licked his cheek.

"Hush, you," Yuugo crossed his arms and said in a tired voice.

Tomoki didn't have a lot of concentration to begin with, but he definitely wouldn't be able to concentrate with a cat and a crow freaking out around him. Yuugo spread his wings wide and flapped them furiously while standing. Jade fell off his shoulder from the wind pressure and tumbled to the ground, and Kurou was thrown backwards in the air.

"Yuugo, that wasn't nice! You could have just asked them to be quiet!" Tomoki held Jade in his arms, who was meowing loudly, and Kurou was perched on his shoulder.

"Yeah, I'll be quiet!"

"Me, too!" They both swore quietly and smiled at Yuugo. He turned away, discouraged. He knew he had lost.

"I can't make a katana like yours." A flickering, blurry image glowed in Tomoki's hands.

"You can't expect things you imagine to materialize at first," Yuugo explained. It seemed like Tomoki wanted a weapon like his a lot more than armor.

"The essence of his spirit seems completely different. Maybe his powers are different from Yuugo's?" Jade said, looking up from the ground.

"I don't know. All I can conjure up is this light in my hand. It happened that one time when I was trying to get away from some demons," Tomoki said dejectedly. As he closed his hands into fists and pushed them out, thin green lines webbed out, firing a faint, shiny membrane around his body. "What is this?"

Jade tried to touch it, but her fur stood up like she had received an electric shock. "Ow!" she cried. Next, Yuugo tried to touch the transparent membrane. There was a snap of energy in his fingertip like static electricity.

"Is this a defensive barrier?"

"Hmm...Lord Tomoki is good at defense. Is he the Barrier Master we have heard about?" Kurou got excited, referring to a rumor he heard from some other demons.

"But aren't Barrier Masters really rare among Dark Walkers?"

"But they said his spiritual energy was green and Lord Tomoki's is a beautiful green..."

"Is a Barrier Master someone who has great defensive powers?" Yuugo asked Kurou, who was confidently pointing at Tomoki.

Hikaru Yura

"That's not at all. They can make 'places' in the human world and send demons to them!"

Tomoki looked annoyed at how excited Kurou was. "Even if that's true, I'd never do that! They'd eat all the humans!" He squeezed his hand, and the green membrane disappeared as if it had melted into the air.

"I hope it's true! Then you can let me live in the other world!"

"And I want to watch TV! And try to transform into a human!"

"I'll turn into a high school girl and dress really cute!" The two of them seemed to really long to go to the human world.

"A Barrier Master, huh..." Yuugo stroked his chin thoughtfully.

Far away on a rocky mountain top, one man stood, looking down at them. "Looks like he's almost awakened." He wore a brown leather jacket. He was at least two meters tall and had long arms and legs. His golden hair flowed down his back like a mane. He had a beautifully chiseled face that was so perfect that it seemed somehow artificial. His cruel blue eyes burned with ambition, and his lips formed a cynical smile. He had strong muscles that had been forged in the heat of battle.

"But that annoying Dark Walker is with him." He stared at the winged Yuugo with a look of amusement on his face. "Looks strong." He chuckled deeply. "Wonder how I should tear him apart and kill him?" He

got excited just thinking about it. He stared at Yuugo, almost like he was evaluating him. "But that's the one I want." He shifted his gaze back to Tomoki. "I see the resemblance," he muttered. Cruel laughter came from his lips.

Once the rainy season started, there was rarely a sunny day. They had switched to the light, short-sleeved school uniforms at the beginning of June. It was very humid, but the temperature wasn't high enough to make one sweat.

Every day, Yuugo would walk to school with Tomoki. And every day, Tomoki would rub his sleepy eyes. Sometimes he would even doze off on Yuugo's shoulder under the umbrella. Yuugo would support the half-asleep Tomoki and hold both their bags and umbrellas.

"Good morning, Oda-kun!"

"Morning, Oda-kun, want me to take his bag?"

"No, I'll wake him up when we get to the shoe lockers." The girls would always greet him quietly so as not to wake up Tomoki, and Yuugo would smile back cheerfully.

"Look, Oda's carrying Tomoki again!" The boys would laugh as they came through the school gate.

"Naruse-kun looks so cute when he's sleeping!"

"That's not a surprise; when he's awake, he looks like a little kid!"

Yuugo's female admirers looked on with difficult looks on their faces. "I wonder if Oda-kun and Naruse-kun are doing it."

"I dunno, maybe he's just being a good friend?"

"Yeah, they don't look like lovers."

"Tomoki, wake up." Yuugo shook him awake when they had reached the shoe lockers.

"Where...am I?" Tomoki asked, confused. He rubbed his eyes sleepily.

"At school in Reality. It's about five minutes before first period." As Yuugo changed his shoes, he handed a stack of letters to Tomoki, who was stretching.

"I don't want your love letters!" Tomoki said, yawning, but reluctantly took them anyway. The lockers next to the classrooms had locks on them, so the girls usually put love letters in the shoe lockers, which did not.

Once, he had seen Yuugo about to throw the letters away and had taken them from him. He knew it took courage to write those letters. Even if Yuugo didn't want to read them, it was too cruel to just throw them away right there.

"Don't throw them away at school!"

"But I'm going out with you!"

Tomoki was happy that Yuugo was being so considerate, but if they ever found out Yuugo had thrown their letters away, the girls would be heartbroken and humiliated. Yuugo wasn't used to other people, so he still didn't have a lot of common sense.

After Tomoki put the stack of letters into his bag, he opened his own shoe locker, and saw there was one letter inside. "Is this...?" The letter was addressed to him, and he blushed. It was the first love letter he had ever gotten!

"Want me to throw it away for you?" Yuugo asked, smiling, and Tomoki quickly shook his head.

"I'll take care of it on the way home."

During class, he read the letter with his heart pounding. It was pretty intense, and closed with, "Please go out with me!" He laid his face down on his desk. Lately, he'd often fall asleep during class, and sometimes even during gym class. Every night in his dreams, Tomoki was training to learn how to protect himself. He was so tired from that that he didn't care where he fell asleep. Once he had fallen asleep on the gymnasium floor, and the guys from the sports club had gathered around him.

"Is he a first year? He's got a pretty face."

"It says he's Tomoki Naruse, from class 1-A!" One of the guys laughed as he read the name tag on Tomoki's gym shirt.

"He looks pretty comfy."

"But isn't that kinda S&M-ish?" The upperclassmen burst out laughing. Yuugo, who had been searching for Tomoki, happened to overhear and curiously peered inside. He was shocked to see that Tomoki had fallen asleep with his hands and feet tangled up in the volleyball net.

"Sorry, this kid is in my class," he had said protectively, pushing through the crowd. He had picked Tomoki up in his arms. As Tomoki rubbed his eyes, their senpai called in disappointed voices, "See ya later, Tomoki Naruse-kun!"

"Come back and sleep again!"

Yuugo's head hurt. When Tomoki was sleeping, his

face looked so sensual and defenseless that it captivated people.

"Y-Y-You...Where do you think you are?" Tomoki yelled at Yuugo behind the school building. "Don't hold me like that at school!"

A boy from another class had called Tomoki out to the hallway, and Yuugo had followed them. He had said "What do you want?" and put an arm around Tomoki's shoulders protectively.

"It was none of your business!" Tomoki pushed his chest.

The boy had clearly wanted to talk about something, but, after Yuugo's behavior, had promptly fled. Other boys standing in the hallway stared at them. "Is he for real?"

"Oh my god, did you just see that?" The boys stared in amazement.

"Gross!"

Hearing their comments, Tomoki had turned pale and looked away. "W-What's the matter with you, you idiot? Now everyone will think we're together!"

Yuugo had tilted his head. "But it's the truth, so what's the problem?"

The problem was that it *was* true! "Because it's not normal for guys to go out with each other. If other people find out, they'll make our lives a living hell until graduation," Tomoki had whispered, frustrated.

"Don't worry, I'll take care of it," Yuugo had said, placing a hand on his shoulder. He had walked over to the group of boys, put his hand on the wall and had a short conversation with them. When he was done, a few of them had turned bright red and scampered away.

What did he do? Tomoki had seen Yuugo's "winning" smile on his face.

"What did you say to them?" Tomoki yelled from behind the school building. "Why are you flirting with other guys?"

"I only flirt with you."

"That smile of yours is a crime!" Yuugo leaned over and pressed him against the wall, silencing his angry lips with a kiss. "Mmph..." His familiar tongue slid into his mouth. His face felt hot and he went weak in the knees.

"You're blushing," Yuugo whispered softly in his ear. He held him tightly, and Tomoki's heart pounded. "I asked them if they were in love with you."

"*What?!*" Tomoki's eyes flew open.

"They were looking at us so enviously."

"Of course they weren't!"

"Then I told them you had gotten a love letter and told them the initials on it. Three of them looked really nervous. I bet they like you." The love letter Tomoki had received only had the sender's initials written on it. It looked very much like a boy's handwriting.

"You're overanalyzing it! You never read the letters, so you probably don't know, but a lot of guys have sent you love letters, too. Maybe those guys really like *you!* It's because you hit on anything that walks that this kind of stuff happens!"

"I don't like being mean to people. I'm not

insensitive like you."

"Insensitive?! Like *you* have any room to talk!" Tomoki cried angrily.

"Sorry. I guess when I think about it, you *are* pretty sensitive, huh?" he smiled sexily, but Tomoki turned his face away. "Tomoki..." Yuugo whispered his name into his ear, and Tomoki froze, as if under a magic spell.

"You're a coward, Yuugo." His wet tongue licked behind Tomoki's ear.

"See, you're sensitive."

"Mmm..."

He playfully bit Tomoki's earlobe, making him moan. He put his large hands on Tomoki's hips and drew him close. Tomoki could feel Yuugo's hardness press against him. He felt himself searching for pleasure, and begin to throb. Yuugo sighed, satisfied, as he propped Tomoki's body up. "It took me a whole year to train you to react this way."

"What?" Tomoki went bright red and yelled. "What do you think I am?"

"My lover."

"Is that something you'd say to your lover?"

"All I did was remember your erogenous zones and use them to my advantage."

"It's the same thing!" Tomoki yelled again. "If you keep doing this to me, my body's gonna be destroyed!"

"It's okay, your body heals faster in the Depths of Dreams. A little wound will heal the next day."

"W-Wound?"

Yuugo laughed and stuck out his tongue.

"I-I hate you!" Tomoki yelled and pushed Yuugo

off. He ran away. He couldn't believe Yuugo just said that to him at school! He was so mad that Yuugo didn't how to act properly at school, but he was even more pissed off that Yuugo said he had "trained" Tomoki and used him to his "advantage."

And even though Yuugo said he was Tomoki's lover, he still smiled that flirty smile at everyone else. That made Tomoki furious. "Yuugo, you idiot!" he yelled as he ran off.

As he dozed off into the Depths of Dreams, Tomoki imagined the ocean. He became a fish swimming through the ocean depths. He fell slowly and pleasantly. He wanted to keep swimming, but once he touched the ground he knew he didn't have wings and he couldn't fly. His body felt lighter here than it did on earth.

Below him, Yuugo waited for him, smiling, with his arms outstretched. Tomoki reached his hands out to his lover happily and Yuugo caught him in his arms. "Tomoki," he called his name gently. Suddenly, Tomoki regained full consciousness.

"Next time you pull that at school, we're breaking up!" Tomoki yelled, clutching his chest. He remembered how mad he had been after school.

"Changing the subject..." Yuugo said, smiling, and put him on the ground.

"No, don't change the subject! It's important!"

"Of course!" Yuugo was smiling, apparently ignoring Tomoki's anger. "We have to think of a schedule so you don't keep falling asleep whenever and wherever you want," he said, crossing his arms in thought.

Luckily, since Tomoki still considered dreams to be things that happened at night, his body didn't disappear when he fell asleep during the day.

"When you enter dreams with your body intact, it's different from your body actually getting to sleep. I can recover with just a few minutes, but you need to sleep at least three more hours to recover."

"I don't know when I'm sleeping and when I'm not. I want to rest, so you need to stop that."

"Stop what?"

"That...thing you do until the morning. It's too rough and it hurts me," Tomoki said quietly, his face red.

"No way. We'll think of another solution."

"Yuugo!" Tomoki yelled and clutched his chest, but Yuugo took advantage of this and kissed him. He tried to push away, but Yuugo's tongue slid deeper into his mouth. Tomoki felt weak and dizzy from the passionate kisses. He felt Yuugo's hardness pushing against him. He unconsciously held onto the base of Yuugo's wings.

"Let's stop practicing for today," Yuugo said, licking his ear. Tomoki's body trembled. "Your clothes are already off, anyway." Yuugo pointed at him. Tomoki hadn't realized that his clothes had disappeared. When he turned around, he saw Jade and Kurou staring at them from the darkness.

"I-I won't interrupt!"

"Me, either!" They both swore in small voices.

"This is all your fault!" Tomoki yelled at Yuugo, his face bright red. He had been holding onto Yuugo before he could imagine his clothes. "Listen – from now on, kissing during practices is forbidden!"

Yuugo reluctantly nodded. It was true that, until Tomoki mastered his powers, this world was too dangerous.

"I can finally make a barrier." Tomoki said. They started to practice on him building up energy in his fist. "The easiest thing to imagine is a yo-yo. I know it's a toy, but I'm pretty good at it," he said. He slowly brought his hand up and then held it up. A beautiful green light followed Tomoki's hand movements. He brought his arm high above his head and like he was holding a magic jewel, a bright golden-green light glowed from his fist. When this light moved to his right hand, he made a fist and held the light. "Like this."

He pulled it up in front of his face, and then pushed it out in front of him. Momentarily his outstretched palm emitted a green ball of light. The small flash pierced through the darkness, and there was a loud sound coming from the other side.

Tomoki lightly raised his middle finger, and the ball returned to his hand with a smacking noise.

"Lord Tomoki! It made a hole in that rock over there!" Kurou had gone to investigate.

"Wow, Tomoki!"

"That's awesome! Actually, I wanted to become a yo-yo pro when I was little," Tomoki said excitedly.

"That was very amazing, but Lord Tomoki can also curse demons with his Flame Fist."

"Are you sure, Kurou?"

"I happened to overhear the demons talking about

it." Apparently Kurou loved to eavesdrop.

"If you're a Barrier Master, they said you can also paralyze people with a curse."

"It's probably better for you to learn that instead of training with a weapon like me," Yuugo said, and Tomoki nodded.

"Yeah, I think you're right."

After that, Tomoki's skills improved, surprising even Yuugo. His abilities grew every day. The barriers that he created could keep most demons away. He could stretch the flexible barrier, and could even make it opaque. It was a defensive power even Yuugo didn't have.

So far he could only curse weak demons, but soon Tomoki could probably learn how to curse tougher enemies like a normal Barrier Master. When that happened, he'd be quite a threat to the demon population. He could make barriers Above Ground, and make a "road" to anywhere else in the world. It would also be possible for him to push demons into the real world.

If Tomoki called a strong demon inside of a barrier made Above Ground, it wouldn't be difficult for them to get out. Would they brutally tear apart the humans and leave their corpses? Or would they devour them without leaving any evidence behind? The flesh of humans was the greatest feast for any demon. High-ranking demons would do anything to get their hands on a Barrier Master so they could get a chance to go to the human world.

In mid June, the days were clear and pleasant. At the end of lunch, the two of them stood by the window in the empty classroom, talking quietly.

"It's not a weapon like yours, but my barriers have gotten better, haven't they?" Tomoki asked in a proud voice. "If I focus the power to my fingertips, I can curse smaller demons." He concentrated on his fingertips, and a small green light about the size of a soap bubble flickered there.

"Yeah, you've gotten really good," Yuugo was genuinely impressed.

"Can you make your katana appear in Reality?" Tomoki asked.

"An illusion of it." He held out both of his hands and stood towards the window. The faint outline of his katana floated in his hands. In the sunlight, it shone a pale rainbow color.

"It's so pretty," Tomoki sighed, as if he were staring at an actual jewel.

"No matter how hard I try, I can't materialize it here." They spoke in hushed voices by the window.

"If you did, you'd probably get arrested."

"That's true."

"But if you dressed up in a costume, they might think you were doing stunts for a movie or something."

"What's that?"

"I'll let you borrow a video later," Tomoki chuckled.

"Hey, are you guys looking at porno magazines or something?" Some of their male classmates called from behind them.

"If they're not, they're doing something awfully suspicious!" Tashiro said, making fun of their secret conversation.

"Tomoki, I have to go meet someone," Yuugo said after school, scratching his head.

"Who?" Tomoki asked, blinking. He started to get worried. They always walked home together, but it seemed like Yuugo didn't want Tomoki to wait for him that day.

"Oh, don't worry. I have to go see my guardian."

"It's not like I thought you were going on a date with a girl or something," Tomoki said, shrugging.

"He wants to talk to me about my grandma's house, so can you go home ahead of me?"

"Yeah, okay." It seemed like Yuugo didn't get along with his guardian.

"When we're done, I'll come over to your house. It's dangerous, so go straight home," Yuugo said, pointing his finger at him.

Tomoki agreed and smiled. Yuugo laughed and messed up his hair, then walked away. "Hey, don't treat me like a kid!" Tomoki laughed as he straightened up his hair. Then, just as Yuugo had told him to, he headed home without taking any detours.

He took the same route home as they always did. When he walked down the main road, it had still been light. But after he turned off towards the residential district, he began to feel a little uneasy. The road was narrow, and on both sides of him houses were surrounded by fences or hedges. It was around dinnertime, so there wasn't anyone outdoors.

Until he had turned down that road, it had been sunset, but all of a sudden it felt like it had grown dark. When he looked back, he saw that the main road was still bright. Maybe it was just an optical illusion?

He hesitantly looked up at the sky and it was dark with no stars, almost like a winter sky. The blue-white light from the street lights illuminated the road. Even though Tomoki knew people lived in those houses, he felt like he was walking down a road that led to a graveyard or something.

Strangely, there wasn't a single insect swarming to the lights.

"When I'm done, I'll come over to your house." He remembered Yuugo's words, sighed, and began walking again. He could see Yuugo's apartment from here. There weren't any lights coming from it. Yuugo would have to come home using this same path.

I wonder where he is. If Yuugo had been walking with him, Tomoki wouldn't have felt so uneasy. Tomoki felt warm from the humid, summer air against his cheeks.

Why weren't there any other people around? As soon as he thought this, Tomoki's body began to tremble. He had goosebumps on his arms. "Was this road always this quiet?" He was lonely because Yuugo wasn't with him. The darkness between the light and the shadows grew deeper.

Frightened, Tomoki clenched his sweaty fist

nervously. Cold sweat soaked his school uniform. Just then, he saw something waving in the darkness. He gasped and then reflexively backed away. "Who's there?" he shouted in a trembling voice. Tomoki's heart pounded, throbbing in his chest. He saw many shadows stand up in the deep darkness. The shadows became silhouettes and came gliding towards him. They had no eyes, noses, or mouths; they were simply black silhouettes.

"Ahhh!" Tomoki's scream was swallowed by the darkness. *They're demons!* He panicked, but tried not to scream. His cold sweat ran into his eyes and he blinked repeatedly. "Damn it...Calm down!" Tomoki chided himself. Yuugo wasn't here, so he'd have to do something himself. Looking behind him, he saw several more creepy shadows standing behind him. Clenching his fist, he stared at the black silhouettes. When he opened his fist, a green globe of light appeared. He punched towards the nearest silhouette and a flash of light raced towards it, then the silhouette disappeared like a popped balloon. When Tomoki moved his fingers again, the beam of light zigzagged through the shadows, cutting them in two.

Should I go? His ball of light had defeated his enemies just as Tomoki had hoped, and it returned to his fist. That was the result of all the special training he'd done in his dreams. He let out a sigh of relief and was looking behind him when a large shadow washed over him like a tidal wave.

"Ahhh!" A sense of great pressure pressed down upon Tomoki and he screamed. Suddenly, the asphalt around his feet began to sink down in the darkness. He tried to endure the enormous weight. *Concentrate!* His body started to glow in the darkness, and then the light collected in his fist. "Yuugo!" he screamed, not because he was crying for help, but to cheer himself on. Tomoki had sunk down to his knees, but just as he thought he'd be crushed his fists emitted a strong flash of light. The explosion echoed in the small alley. It pierced through the ceiling of darkness, and then a beam of bright golden-green light smashed the darkness into small pieces. Tomoki's ears rang from the noise, and his vision went white.

The night air caressed Tomoki, who was lying on the ground.

"Are you okay?" He opened his eyes at the sound of Yuugo's voice, and they spun from the flickering red and yellow lights.

"Did you just save me, Yuugo?" Tomoki clutched Yuugo's shirt and whispered, dazed. He looked up at Yuugo's face, but still hadn't fully regained his vision.

"No, that was your power." As he picked Tomoki up, Yuugo let out a slow sigh. When he had turned off the main road, Yuugo had also felt that feeling of uneasiness. He was worried about Tomoki, so he had run through the wall of darkness at the very moment it had been destroyed in a flash of green light. "You really are a Barrier Master."

"I did it by myself?"

"Yeah," Yuugo whispered, and Tomoki blinked and

looked at his fist. "But now I know for sure that there are demons coming to Reality," Yuugo said seriously as he held Tomoki. "And they're after you."

"Me?"

"Probably." Tomoki gulped as he saw the worried look on Yuugo's face. "What I don't understand is how they can get near you if you're a Barrier Master." Tomoki felt like he could hear Yuugo's uneasiness, even though he didn't say anything about it.

"That demon bitch..." Kanon growled as he walked down the hallway. "She'll keep calling me that terrible name until I defeat her." He was talking about Shana, a beautiful female demon who took on the form of a seven-year-old girl with long, silver hair. She was actually a few thousand years old, and she controlled the Depths of Dreams as the Queen of the Underworld. She was proud of her immense power, and played with people's hearts and souls to pass the time.

"I haven't seen you in a while, Lump of Mud," Shana had said to Kanon when he kneeled before her throne. "Who are you again, Mud?" The girl wore a white lace dress and smiled coldly. She was beautiful, but her expression was not that of a young girl. She was the Queen of the Underworld, and had limitless power and pride.

"You gave me the name 'Kanon,' Queen Shana," he had answered.

"Look at me." Inside, Kanon had been startled, but did not let it show on his face as he looked up at the silver-haired girl. "Yes, that's right. I named you after a blond, blue-eyed man. I had a lot of fun with him...before I ate him. But your face and body are more beautiful. That's because I mixed together mud and human and demon to create you."

"Yes, thank you, Queen Shana."

"Do not thank me. Just remember: if you are of no use to me, I will send you back to the earth from which you came," the girl had said, narrowing her eyes and tightening her lips. "I don't care what you think. I gave you your orders, and you know what will happen if you disobey them."

"Yes, Queen Shana." Her sticky-sweet voice had struck him to the core. When their eyes had met for just a second, she had not seen the wild ambition in his.

"I'll kill that demon bitch and obtain eternal life!" Shana had no idea about his ambitions. She had no interest in what the creature she had made was thinking. Shana survived with her demon instincts, and she did not possess an ounce of love or mercy. She had created talking dolls to pass the time of her long existence, and if they were of use to her she did not destroy them. That was as far as it went. If he showed an inkling of disobedience, Kanon knew she would destroy him in an instant.

"Damn you, Shana," Kanon spat as he headed towards his own castle. "There's no female Dark Walkers!" Shana had ordered Kanon to search for women many times. He was supposed to present this legendary woman, who only appeared once every thousand years or something, to "Queen Shana." He didn't know if she wanted to sacrifice the Dark Walker to increase her own power, or if she was some kind of messiah to the humans. Either way, he had no use for her.

But he didn't know when Shana might return him to the earth on one of her whims. He wanted the power to defeat her.

"That's why I need the Dark Walker who's a Barrier Master!" Remembering the slave he had hidden away in his castle, Kanon started to laugh. "And I found another one like him, too." The new one was the young boy who had recently come to the Depths of Dreams, Tomoki Naruse. If he combined both of their powers together, a very powerful Barrier Master could be created. Until now, Kanon's slave had made small barriers to send himself and other demons to Reality. But what if Kanon combined both their strengths? He could seal Shana for all eternity, and obtain the power to destroy the boundary between the Depths of Dreams and Reality.

"My power as a Creator shall exceed even Shana's!" He laughed in a menacingly low voice. In the corner of his light blue eyes, the flame of ambition sparkled.

On the way home, Yuugo brought Tomoki off the main road and headed towards a brightly lit business district. The end of August was approaching. It had rained since early afternoon, so it was a bit humid outside now into the evening.

"Can you wait there, Tomoki?" He pointed towards

a bright arcade.

"Is something here?" Tomoki looked up anxiously, but Yuugo shook his head.

"I need to stop by somewhere. Just go play. And don't leave the brightness."

"Okay," Tomoki agreed, nodding.

Yuugo watched Tomoki enter the bright arcade, and then quickly looked behind him. On the other side of the dark alleyway, the figure of the woman who had been staring at them had disappeared into the shadows. She wasn't human. He could tell by her silhouette that she had very long hair, and the only thing that was clear was her glittering red eyes. "Is she after Tomoki?" He ran towards the back of the alleyway.

"It's been a long time since I've been to an arcade!" It was bustling even on a weeknight. When Tomoki was in junior high, he often came there to check out the new games—but he hadn't been since he started high school.

"Oh, they got a new version of this one!" Tomoki sat in front of a familiar fighting game and put a coin in. Tomoki never played as female characters in video games. It looked too painful when they got punched by men and he felt sorry for them. He decided to play as a muscular, powerful-looking young man. Tomoki liked playing as someone who was the complete opposite of who he was in Reality. As he easily defeated his opponents, Tomoki continued to advance to the next level. He fought a tall man who resembled Yuugo, and smiled as he easily defeated him.

What was strange was that he didn't get as excited about the character's battles as he did before. "Yuugo is way better!" Since Tomoki had seen him fight a real battle, he thought there wasn't anyone as strong as Yuugo. "But I wonder how he is in Reality?" He had never seen Yuugo fight in real life, so he wasn't sure. Yuugo looked like he had a slim body, but when he took his clothes off they revealed an amazing, muscular body. His face went bright red thinking about it.

"Hey, you're pretty good," he heard a voice say over his shoulder as he entered his initials into the high score screen. "That game looks fun." Tomoki looked up from the screen. There was a young man standing behind Tomoki with golden hair and blue eyes, about twenty-five years old, wearing a brown leather jacket. His chiseled face was beautiful, yet masculine. He had long arms and legs and broad shoulders. He was at least two meters tall, taller than Yuugo. His blond hair shone and flowed down his back like a mane. It was almost like he had stepped out of one of the arcade games.

Maybe he's a model who came to Japan?

"If I'm not bothering you, can I watch you play some more?"

"What?" Tomoki asked as the man leaned over and smiled.

"I'm Kanon. What's your name?"

"Kanon-san? I'm Tomoki Naruse," Tomoki introduced himself shyly. Kanon's light blue eyes shone with satisfaction.

Tomoki started playing the same game again,

while Kanon leaned over him and watched. At first it was awkward, but then Kanon began to ask him various questions about the game.

"Your Japanese is good," Tomoki said, making Kanon smile.

"I live with my Japanese lover," the corner of his lips curled up meaningfully, but Tomoki didn't notice.

"Tomoki!" Yuugo yelled as he crossed the arcade. Tomoki and all of the customers turned around and stared. "Get away from him!"

"What?" Tomoki asked, standing up. He looked from the blond man to Yuugo.

"He's a jealous guy, huh?" Kanon laughed, putting a hand on Tomoki's shoulder. Tomoki stiffened under his touch.

"Don't touch him!"

"Don't tell me what to do!" Kanon snapped back at Yuugo's angry voice. He walked towards Yuugo slowly. They didn't take their eyes of each other. The atmosphere inside the arcade was tense, and the other customers looked on nervously.

Kanon was the first to look away. With a smile on his face, he headed towards the nearby exit. "Dark Walker," he whispered in Yuugo's ear. "Your precious Tomoki will soon be mine." When Yuugo turned around, Kanon had already disappeared through the automatic doors. He rushed after him and looked up and down the street, but he was nowhere to be seen.

"Damn it!"

Tomoki rushed over to him. "What's wrong?"

"He's not human." Yuugo grabbed Tomoki and

pulled him close. "He's a demon!"

Kanon's castle was in the heart of a steep, rocky mountain in the Depths of Dreams. The interior was spacious and the rooms were decorated extravagantly, but somehow the balance seemed off. The resident had no attachment to it, and the castle had an empty grandeur about it.

Deep inside the castle was a hidden room. It was the most elaborately furnished room of them all. It had a bedroom, living room, and bathroom. The finest garments hung in the closet, and there was a large, canopied bed.

This was the only world Shiki knew. When he was alone in the quiet room, it felt cold. The sound of his clothes rustling and his footsteps echoed.

The only one who would come in was his master, Kanon. No one else existed in Shiki's world.

Master Kanon should be home soon, he thought as he stood near the door. The Chinese-style clothes he wore were knee-length and magnificently embroidered. Shiki had a beautiful face. His brown eyes always had a sad cast to them. His perfect lips were glossy and light pink. He moved elegantly with a quiet manner. His chestnut-colored hair was silky and shoulder-length. Shiki's white skin had never seen the sun since he lived in this world, but he didn't look unhealthy. Instead, his pale skin had a pearly glow about it.

Shiki had been taken captive by Kanon when he was a child, and had been cultivated into a powerful

Barrier Master in a short time. For about two years, he had been drifting inside a vat filled with warm liquid that resembled amniotic fluid. During that time, all Shiki did was gaze at Kanon's blue eyes. After Kanon let him out, Shiki had been his slave ever since. Kanon was his only master in this small world Shiki had been given.

He didn't know whether it was an unhappy thing or not. Shiki couldn't remember when he had been kidnapped. Around Shiki's right wrist was a golden bracelet set with a sparkling blue jewel. It looked good on him. It was a demon crystal Kanon had created, and it was the same cold blue as his eyes. The jewel increased Shiki's powers.

"Master Kanon is home!" he said from the bedside table. Since there were no windows in the room, he spent most of his time gazing into the crystal ball. With it, he could see where his master was and make a barrier anywhere in Reality to send Kanon there.

Sometimes he would watch his parents and brother through Kanon's eyes. His younger brother, Tomoki, had grown up, but it seemed like he was far away in a foreign country.

Tomoki...he whispered his brother's name. He was only one year old when Shiki had been taken captive. Shiki remembered how happy he was when his mother had let him hold his baby brother. He would rub his cheek on Tomoki's and hold his little hand. Shiki remembered his soft skin that always smelled like milk. Shiki had only lived with him for a year, and Tomoki was just beginning to talk when Shiki had been taken captive.

Shiki had tried everything to be sure, from the

faraway land of dreams, that Tomoki wouldn't awaken as a Barrier Master. If he was a Dark Walker, he must never awaken. If he did, Kanon would find him, and kidnap him. Or he would eaten by demons in the Depths of Dreams. But it hadn't worked. "If he doesn't awaken, he might be able to live a happy life." The worst case scenario was that Tomoki was a Barrier Master like Shiki. His only relief was that Tomoki had someone else to protect him. Tomoki's protector was one of the strongest among the Dark Walkers. But Shiki wasn't sure if a human could stand against Kanon.

"I wish it was just me..." Shiki whispered, thinking of his little brother. A tear trickled down Shiki's cheek and fell onto his hand.

Kanon walked quickly down the red carpeted hallway to the large double doors in the back of the castle. The moment Kanon placed both hands on the door, orange sparks fired. The doors were made so that only Kanon's hands could unlock them.

"Welcome home, Master Kanon!" Beyond the doors stood the beautiful young boy Kanon had captured. Seeing the angry look on his face, Shiki unconsciously backed away.

"Did you find her?"

"No, I didn't see her in the crystal ball," Shiki shook his head at Kanon's question.

"Humph. Whatever." Kanon flopped down on the leather couch and crossed his legs. He drank the strong alcohol Shiki had prepared for him. He could feel the heat of the alcohol traveling down into his stomach.

Kanon's body had been created for Shana's

amusement, mixing human and demon. Because he was part human, Kanon had feelings. Sometimes, those feelings were incomprehensible to him. Anxiety and fear. But the demon in him was insensitive and never attempted to validate those feelings. "Shana can't find her, either." It was said there was a female Dark Walker every thousand years or so, and Shana was waiting for her.

"Just a little longer. Just a little bit longer, and I'll defeat that bitch and become immortal. And when I do, the whole world will be mine!"

"Master Kanon." Shiki began to grow frightened.

"That bitch called me a lump of mud again." Shana made Kanon, and he didn't have a real life as a demon. She could create lives and destroy them. Then the only thing left of them was flesh and mud. "She called *me* that!" He squeezed the earthenware cup violently, and it shattered into tiny pieces in his hands, making him even angrier.

"Master Kanon."

Kanon thought this feeling he had that made his fists shake was called "anger."

Shiki unconsciously went to embrace Kanon and held onto his clothes. "Shall I comfort you, Master?"

"What right do you have, as a slave, to pity me?" Kanon's eyes burned with anger, and Shiki shook his head. "What? The human pities the lump of mud?"

"No, that's not..." Kanon lifted him off the ground by his collar and Shiki clung to his arm. His feet were far from the floor and he couldn't breathe. His master threw Shiki down violently onto the large bed, and his body bounced. He tried to get away, but Kanon held him down. A groan of pain escaped him.

"My blood is black, so I want to see your red blood." Kanon stripped off his own clothes and dug his nails into Shiki's skin.

"Ahhh!"

Shiki's clothes were ripped from left to right, his bare skin exposed. Kanon made one cruel red mark all the way from the back of his neck to his hips. The lights in the bedroom had a soft, warm hue. But the indirect lighting on the walls illuminated Shiki's body like a spotlight. He was stripped of all his clothes except for his boots, and made to lie face down on the bed.

"Master Kanon, please forgive me..." Shiki felt cold leather straps binding his arms behind his back. The blue jewel on his bracelet sparkled the same blue as Kanon's eyes.

Kanon had found him fourteen years earlier, when Shiki had first come to the Depths of Dreams. He had been a nine-year-old at the time, still wearing his pajamas. Shiki had been wandering about the desolate landscape with an anxious look on his face. The demons had silently retreated into the darkness when they saw the pale green light like a burning flame that enveloped the boy's body. They knew that was the color of a Barrier Master. He hadn't fully awakened yet, but still no demon could get near him.

The boy had disappeared into the darkness, possibly because he had awakened again in Reality.

After that, Kanon had waited for Shiki to return. He was a Barrier Master who could travel freely through the strata of the Depths of Dreams. If Kanon got ahold of Shiki, he would be able to go the the human world whenever he pleased. He wanted to see the world Above Ground, where it was said swarms of humans and their delicious flesh lived. But what Kanon wanted most of all was to defeat that bitch Shana, and to solidify his very existence.

At sunset, a golden wave had washed ashore. The boy was playing on the beach away from his parents when suddenly a tall man stood above him. Shiki couldn't make out the man's face clearly in the sunlight. All Shiki could see were his light blue eyes. His long, beautiful golden hair fluttered in the sunlight. He smiled gently at Shiki, and the boy blushed and smiled back brightly. That's all Shiki remembered of the world Above Ground.

Then he was inside the clear cylindrical tank, staring dreamily at Kanon.

Kanon. As he watched Shiki grow from a boy to a young man, he became more fascinated with the beautiful creature's body each passing day.

"I've had sex with many women Above Ground, but your skin is the most beautiful I've ever seen." He stroked Shiki's back with a finger, and narrowed his eyes with satisfaction. His slave's skin had rarely seen the sun, and it was smooth and pearl-white. Among all the people Kanon had had sex with or killed, Shiki was the most beautiful.

The sight of his bound, naked body was so erotic it made Kanon shiver. He desired the human male part of his body. "It makes me want to tear you apart and eat you," he whispered in a low voice. Demons loved the flesh right underneath soft skin. They loved slitting human's bellies and burying their faces inside their warm flesh. But Kanon couldn't eat this one, for Shiki was his valuable pawn. The more he suppressed his hunger, the more Kanon's desire for Shiki rose.

"Lick it." Kanon stood beside the bed and grabbed Shiki's head.

"Master Kanon," Shiki looked up at him with wet eyes. "I'll service you, but please untie me," he pleaded with his master as Kanon shoved his erection in front of his face.

"Use your tongue like I taught you," Kanon ordered him slowly, a cold smile on his face. Shiki slowly took Kanon's thick rod into his mouth. "Just do as I tell you."

"Yes, Master." All Shiki could do was obey. Kanon's member was throbbing before him, and liquid dripped from the tip of it. Shiki kissed Kanon's arousal and licked it neatly as if he was cleaning it. Kanon's raw male taste spread throughout Shiki's mouth. Shiki desperately serviced Kanon with his tongue and his lips as he clutched Shiki's hair. Kanon watched with a cruel smile on his face and then suddenly thrust himself deep into Shiki's mouth.

"Mmph," Shiki grimaced as Kanon's penis plunged into the back of his throat.

"Don't use your teeth!" Kanon yelled. Since he had forced himself into Shiki's mouth, drool dripped down to the boy's chin. He couldn't breathe. Tears flowed from his closed eyes. Kanon withdrew his rod from Shiki's mouth and then blew his cloudy demon cum all over Shiki's face.

"Ahhh!" The liquid poured into his half-open mouth. Shiki drank his master's semen and panted. His body trembled. Even though it was painful, the taste of a demon's cum on his tongue spread through him like an aphrodisiac. Kanon gave a satisfied laugh. He loved getting the pure-looking Shiki filthy and raping him. He had trained Shiki not to disobey him, and had been having sex with him for fourteen years. He held Shiki's restrained body against his chest. He grasped his soft, brown hair and felt Shiki's body tremble. As he saw that Shiki was about to cry, Kanon plunged his tongue into his open mouth.

"Master...Master..." Shiki moaned in a muffled voice, and his closed eyelids trembled. His body became flushed, and he got goosebumps. Saliva poured from the corners of his lips, which Kanon licked up greedily.

Kanon grew hard again just from his kisses, and he pinned Shiki down. He bit the nape of his neck. Tears flowed from Shiki's eyes, and he fought against his restraints. Kanon sucked on his neck noisily, and traced his finger down to the soft flesh of Shiki's ass. He entered his hidden place, and his sharp nails stroked Shiki on the inside. Shiki buried his face and groaned.

He knew it would hurt for days afterward.

"Shiki, open your eyes," Kanon ordered, sitting up. "If you faint, you're gonna get it."

Shiki slightly opened his eyes and looked at Kanon painfully. Seeing Kanon was erect again, his body unconsciously writhed, trying to escape. Kanon spread Shiki's knees wide. "Answer me."

"Yes, Master," Shiki answered quietly, and Kanon was suddenly overcome with a strong desire. At the same time, this made him angry. He would soon grow tired of others, but why did he want Shiki so badly? Was it because, Kanon would never find a more beautiful human, even if he searched all over Above Ground? It was his eyes. His amber eyes, full of sadness, that looked like they had given up everything. He had trained Shiki to never disobey him for fear that Kanon would rip him apart. His slave knew that if he tried to run away, he would find only his own death. But those eyes that stared at Kanon were full of pity.

He couldn't take it!

"Ahhh!" Shiki screamed from the intense pain as Kanon thrust into him at full force. After a while, the pain had subsided just a little. Kanon pulled his hips back and withdrew his thick, hard member. Shiki's breath became shallow. The blood that flowed from Shiki had made Kanon's erection smooth and it slid in easily. He propped one of Shiki's legs up on his shoulder and pushed himself in again. Shiki's legs trembled weakly; his hands, still tied behind his back, had gone numb from the weight of Kanon on top of him.

Just as demon cum started pouring inside of him,

Shiki felt his insides throb. His pain had transformed into dizzying pleasure. "It works better than an aphrodisiac." He blushed at Kanon's voice in his ear. As he slowly moved his hips, Kanon's long fingers wrapped around Shiki's erection. He stroked its wet head with his fingers and massaged the pulsating shaft.

"Master...Master Kanon!" Shiki moaned tearfully. Those gentle caresses were like torture. Just as he had been on the verge of coming, Kanon had roughly grasped the base of his cock. Shiki shook his head. He felt like he would go mad from the pleasure. His aroused body wanted a release. Kanon licked his erect pink nipples, eliciting a tearful scream. Covered in sweat and panting, his sensitive body reacted to everything.

Kanon was still inside Shiki as he lay face down. As he grasped Shiki's member, he forced his body up. He lifted up Shiki's ass. Kanon pulled out his hard rod and it overflowed with demon cum, tinged pink with blood. Shiki's thighs were covered with warm liquid. He felt Kanon watching him, and his cheeks flushed. But his desire was throbbing inside of Kanon's hands. Kanon put his head against Shiki's opening again, and Shiki's body trembled.

"Ahhh!" Kanon thrust himself in all the way down to the base, which caused Shiki to release into Kanon's hand.

"Mmph!" Kanon dug his nails into Shiki's sensitive head and a sharp pain pierced through him.

"Shiki" Kanon called his name into his hot ear. Shiki's body felt weak.

No matter what cruel things Kanon did to him now, it didn't matter —Shiki felt faint, anyway.

"Open your eyes, Shiki," Kanon bit his earlobe and Shiki moaned loudly. He untied the restraints from Shiki's arms and turned his body over. He tied his arms to the bedposts. Kanon's lips twisted cruelly as he grabbed Shiki's ankles and spread them wide apart. His tongue peeked out lewdly from his mouth. His eyes glittered with desire. Kanon felt himself getting hard again. Shiki lay vulnerable in front of him, and his body grew hot and his breathing rough.

"I want you to watch what I do to you."

"Yes, Master," Shiki answered with trembling lips.

Kanon pressed his hard thick head against the boy. Shiki automatically writhed into his leather restraints. Like a hungry beast, Kanon indulged in Shiki over and over again until he grew tired.

Shiki squirmed under Kanon's tongue, which licked his entire body, and came over and over again. His exhausted body wouldn't stop. He stared at Kanon's cruel blue eyes and let out painful moans.

Shiki didn't know if demon semen really was an aphrodisiac. Then again, he didn't know anything when he was being raped.

He couldn't disobey the humiliating pleasure and pain Kanon gave him. That was how his master had trained him. But even though he had to be more powerful than Shiki, Kanon would always tie Shiki up when he raped him. To make Shiki know that he was merely a slave, and that he must never disobey Kanon. Shiki knew that Kanon had immense hatred inside of him. He knew that Shana had created him for her own amusement, and his existence was more uncertain than those demons who wandered the Depths of Dreams. Shana could destroy his beautiful body on a whim. Shiki knew Kanon feared that. The anger he thought he felt was actually fear.

That's why Kanon couldn't forgive his slave for pitying him. He hated everyone that had been given a body of flesh and blood—that had been given a real life.

But it wasn't pity Shiki felt for Kanon...He looked up at Kanon sadly. If he said what he really felt, even if he was necessary because he was a Barrier Master, he knew Kanon would kill him out of anger. But sometimes Kanon would show him his human side. His attachment to him.

"Master Kanon..." Shiki whispered sleepily, and Kanon kissed him preciously.

Free of his restraints, Shiki spread his arms out on top of the sheets. His wrists were bright red, his body exhausted. He couldn't move even if he tried. He absently stared at his fingers as his circulation came back. The room was quiet once more. Shiki could feel warm breath on his hair. He lay in Kanon's arms with his head on Kanon's chest. Kanon's strong arms were wrapped around him.

"You're my slave."

"Yes, Master," he answered. Kanon stroked Shiki's soft skin as if he were petting a dog.

"I'll give you your brother's power."

"..."

Kanon grabbed Shiki's face roughly and turned it towards him. "Answer me, slave. Do not disobey me." Shiki grimaced at the threatening tone in his voice.

"Yes, Master," he answered hoarsely. Kanon licked his pale lips with satisfaction.

"When I have the two of you, I'll have power equal to Shana's." Kanon talked about his terrible plan softly, as if it were regular pillow talk between lovers. "First I'll use you to destroy the world they live in..."

The world welcomed a peaceful July. Around town, there were posters of tanned girls wearing swimsuits everywhere. At dusk, it was about the time the streetlights would flicker on. Train stations and department stores were crowded. Bustling shopping districts were brimming with businessmen, housewives, and students.

The heat of the day rose from the asphalt, making the air moist. Walking amidst the crowd, one could build up a light sweat. It was a regular summertime scene.

"It's been a while since we walked around here," Tomoki said happily as they walked side by side. Lately the days had been uneventful and peaceful. He was still training in the Depths of Dreams, but in Reality he was enjoying his summer vacation. "Let's go visit your house in Shikoku this summer."

"No way," Yuugo said, irritated.

"I know you don't have any good memories of it, but are you sure you don't want to visit your grandma's grave?"

"My guardian takes care of it."

"I want to see where you grew up," Tomoki said. Yuugo scratched his head, looking a little embarrassed.

"There's no TV or games there."

"It's okay, we'll be on vacation. And we'll be together," Tomoki said, his eyes sparkling.

Yuugo didn't feel any nostalgia for the house he had lived in for ten years. He spent most of his time in the Depths of Dreams, so he didn't have any particularly good memories of Reality.

"We'll be busy next year, so we should have lots of fun this summer. We should take a train that stops at every station so we can visit other places, too."

"Yeah," Yuugo answered with a smile.

Tomoki's plan sounded refreshingly normal. Yuugo didn't spend too much time studying, but it seemed like Tomoki wanted to start preparing for college entrance exams next year. The more he hung out with Tomoki and talked, the more Yuugo felt like a normal high school student. He began to think he might be able to live a happy, normal life with Tomoki, like they were just two ordinary students with no powers. Maybe if he went with Tomoki, he'd see his old house in a different light.

"Just make sure you don't hit on anyone else during our trip!" Tomoki said.

"You're the one I have to worry about, now!" Yuugo laughed and pointed at Tomoki.

Sometimes when they'd walk around in their regular clothes, Tomoki would be the one to get hit on.

"Anyway, don't be nice to everyone you see!"

"Why, is that bad?" Even though they would

sometimes quarrel, they'd always make up quickly. As Tomoki discussed the plains for their trip, Yuugo listened agreeably. Suddenly he felt his arm grow heavy, and looked down at it.

"Yuugo..." Tomoki clapped a hand over his mouth. The faint outlines of Yuugo's arm guards started to appear on his arms.

"Why? We're in Reality." Yuugo stared at his arms, dumbfounded. The basketball shoes he had just been wearing changed into boots with metal guards on them. *My body's doing it on its own. But, this is Reality.*

"Why?"

"I dunno," Yuugo said, shaking his head. For a moment, he was unsure of whether this was a dream or reality. Was his power starting to go out of his control? A cold sweat covered his body. *Am I gonna turn into a monster here in the real world?*

"Calm down, Yuugo." Tomoki clutched Yuugo's arm anxiously.

Yuugo's silver arm guards reflected the bright lights coming from the display windows. They felt hard, cold, and real. The armor Yuugo had created in the Depths of Dreams had materialized in Reality.

"But, that's for when you fight." Just as Tomoki said this, a terribly loud noise came from behind them. "Yuugo!" Screams came from all directions and Tomoki turned him around.

A giant horn had torn up through the pavement, completely destroying a nearby bus terminal in the process. It was a demon. It had red-brown fur and horns coming from its head like a bull, but its lower half was human. Its eyes shone an ominous red.

It was an ugly monster that looked like it had been created from a mixture of many creatures. It was much larger than the ten-meter-high sculpture by the train station.

"Ahhh!" Tomoki screamed as one of its giant horns came down towards him. At that moment he heard a flapping sound, and Yuugo carried him high into the sky. "Yuugo, your wings!" Tomoki said, dumbfounded. He was surprised that a demon had appeared there, but also surprised Yuugo could fly Above Ground. Tomoki had thought their powers were just an illusion in Reality, like when Yuugo had tried to make his katana appear in the classroom.

"Shit!" Yuugo roared as a pattern started to materialize on his face. His instincts had taken over and his body was changing on its own. "Someone made a huge barrier!" It looked like there was an invisible barrier in the sky. Even when Yuugo tried to fly away, he couldn't go any higher than the department store.

People below were screaming and running from the hideous monster. Its red eyes gazed at Yuugo as it trampled on the people below, crushing them like ants. Other people ran to escape the same fate, but the monster would just mow them down with its horns. It was an effortless slaughter.

It was literally hell on earth. The sound of ambulance and fire truck sirens rang out. There were flashes of light everywhere, and people took pictures of Yuugo from windows and rooftops.

"Yuugo, look..." Tomoki said, pointing a trembling

finger to the building.

The JumboTron, usually used for advertisements, was showing a black-winged Yuugo carrying Tomoki. Yuugo's bold tiger-stripe war paint had materialized on his face. "Is that me?" Yuugo asked quietly, seeing his transformed body for the first time. "I look just like a demon!" he roared.

"C-Calm down!" Tomoki said, clinging to Yuugo's body and trembling. His anxious face stared back at him from the giant screen.

Tomoki's face looked like he was also searching for help from the demons. Many people were watching them from the windows and roofs of buildings. Their eyes were full of fear, disgust, and anger at the tragedy that was unfolding on the ground.

"Monster!!"

"Demon!!"

Some people even tried throwing things at the demon from nearby buildings. They could hear anguished, chaotic screams from people who had fallen into panic. The winged Yuugo appeared to be the same as the giant monster in their eyes.

"Let go of that boy!" They seemed to think Yuugo had captured Tomoki.

"No, that's not it! No!" Tomoki shook his head and cried, clinging onto Yuugo protectively. Suddenly, they heard gunshots from below them and a bullet grazed one of Yuugo's wings. Policemen were firing from the window of one of the buildings. Yuugo glared at them. The policemen set down their weapons, screamed, and pulled back. They had been trying to save a boy they

thought was a hostage, but they didn't realize that if they shot Yuugo down, Tomoki would tumble to the ground with him.

Yuugo quickly flew around and set Tomoki down on the safest looking rooftop. "It's dangerous, so do *not* leave this spot," he said worriedly, placing a hand on Yomoki's cheek. Tomoki nodded.

"Sleeping Demon Tremor!" Yuugo cried, kicking off the building. "Come! Jade Thunder!" The glittering sword appeared in his hands.

"Yuugo..."

Tomoki couldn't get over the strangeness of the scene before him. The city was the familiar "Real World," and yet Yuugo was holding a sword that had appeared out of nowhere, right before Tomoki's eyes. His hair flew in his face from the wind caused by Yuugo's giant wings. With the setting sun in the background, the building was sinking into darkness. It was ominous and beautiful at the same time.

"Yuugo, be careful!" Tomoki cried, and Yuugo nodded.

He gripped his katana in both hands, and swooped down above the demon. Tomoki watched as a heroic battle between the demon and Yuugo unfolded beneath him. The police and Special Forces had been dispatched. Soon, they would probably call in the Self Defense Forces, too. The barrier was stretched around the entire city. More demons were probably on their way. On the JumboTron, a nervous-looking reporter relayed the details of the "Demon Battle" that was going on.

"They think Yuugo is an evil demon!" Tomoki

clenched his fists.

"Well, isn't this exciting?" a low voice said from behind Tomoki.

"You're...!"

"Isn't that your boyfriend? There's no way he can stay Above Ground, now." Kanon stood atop the building's water tower behind him, arms crossed and smiling. "The humans think this is a fight between demons. He should be able to beat a monster of that caliber, but do you really think that, after this massacre, he'll be seen as the hero who defeated the demon that attacked the city? He has black wings, you know. Not exactly the symbol of a good guy." Kanon spoke casually, his golden hair fluttering in the wind.

"Remove the barrier!" Tomoki screamed angrily, trembling.

Kanon jumped off the tower, not making a sound. "Sorry, little boy. I'm not a first class 'Dark Walker' Barrier Master like you. I can't make barriers. All I am is a lump of mud Shana created." He pulled Tomoki close to him and peered at him. "Wanna know who made it?" He licked Tomoki's cheek, making him shudder. "Shiki did. Your older brother. He's a Barrier Master, too. I'm sure you don't remember what he looks like. Humans that are related not only look alike, but they smell alike, too ... Mmm, it drives me crazy," he whispered excitedly into Tomoki's ear. He licked the nape of Tomoki's neck, and Tomoki clenched his teeth.

That was the first time he had heard that his brother was still alive. *There's no way my brother did this...Kanon has to be behind it!* Had his brother been held captive by Kanon somewhere in the Depths of Dreams? Even though Tomoki didn't remember him that well, he wanted to see his brother very badly.

"As soon as I have both of you, I'll seal Shana and the whole world will be mine!"

"You did this terrible thing just to capture me?"

"Is it really that terrible?" Kanon asked patronizingly. "Just so you know, I'm going to kill you soon—and I don't feel the least bit bad about it," he whispered with a terrifyingly gentle smile on his face. "Anyway, when I obtain your powers, the boundary between the real world and the dream world will vanish. I'll fuse you and Shiki together. If any of your consciousness survives, then you can admire they way I'm gonna destroy this world. And a new world will be born where demons walk and feed on humans."

"Fuse me and my brother?"

"I'm going to give all your powers to Shiki. To the gentle, obedient Shiki. Well, it's about time to start on my masterpiece..." Suddenly, a snap of electricity came from Kanon's finger.

"Don't touch me!" Tomoki glared at his blue eyes, and pushed his fists out.

"Ohh, so it looks like you can make barriers now, huh?" Kanon smiled with an impressed look on his face. A faint green membrane surrounded Tomoki's body, but it was unstable. If Kanon tried to penetrate it, it wouldn't stand a chance against him.

"Get away from me!" Tomoki slowly backed away and put both arms in front of his chest. He concentrated the electric current to his hands and sparks fell.

"Your boyfriend just died."

"What?" Tomoki's eyes flew open as Kanon looked down below them. At that moment, he breached the barrier and grabbed Tomoki with his large hand. "Damn it!" Green sparks burst from Tomoki's fists and landed on Kanon's leather jacket. The demon grimaced slightly and threw Tomoki down.

"Humph. Fine. I'll come back after I get him. Wait here and stay quiet. After all, there's nowhere you can run to," Kanon said, smiling, and walked away. After the sight of his fluttering golden hair vanished, Tomoki rushed over to the side of the building. "Yuugo's in trouble!"

Below him, Yuugo was about to stab one of the demon's arms, but he looked like he was in bad condition as well. As he dodged the demon's attacks, it would toss aside and destroy buildings and houses like toys. If Yuugo didn't dodge its attacks he would surely die, but because of this the collateral damage had intensified.

"Is that...?" Tomoki said as something suddenly caught his eye. "Shiki!" Even though the humans on the ground below seemed like miniatures from this high, he was sure it was his brother. His face looked sad. They definitely looked alike. Tomoki felt a strong sense of nostalgia for his long-lost brother. He started to run down the building's fire escape. "Shiki!"

"Tomoki..." Shiki said as Tomoki ran over to him.

"Don't listen to that demon! Undo the barrier!"

Shiki stood amidst the panicked crowd with his eyes down. He wore an elegant silk shirt, black pants, and boots. A faint green sphere floated above his outstretched hands. That small sphere was what had caused this chaotic scene in Reality.

"You don't really want to do this!" Tomoki yelled, grabbing Shiki's arm. "Oniisan!" The moment he yelled this, the outline of the barrier sphere Shiki held faded. Tomoki held his arms out to him, and suddenly a strong flash of light like a thunderbolt shone between them. The world shook beneath them. "Did...the barrier break?" The moment he felt the tremors, Tomoki's field of vision went black.

Across from Yuugo, the outline of the angry demon that was trampling humans also became faint. Both Yuugo and Kanon, who stood beside him, disappeared like an illusion. The people who witnessed this stared, dumbfounded, as if time had frozen. Even though it had seemed like a dream or an illusion, the harsh reality was still left before them. The buildings the demon had destroyed, the numerous corpses it had left behind—one could hear groans and screams from those who had managed to survive.

As soon as they entered the Depths of Dreams, Yuugo severed the giant demon's head and killed it.

"You look pretty rough," Kanon said as he stared at the panting Yuugo.

Yuugo wiped the blood that streamed from his forehead and shook the blood off the blade of his katana, which glittered in the hazy world of dreams.

"Let me play with you a while," Kanon stretched out his arms. A long saber appeared in his hands. He gripped the handle and swung it through the air with a whirring noise. As he held it before him, it reflected his cold, blue eyes. "Dark Walker," he whispered and lunged at Yuugo.

Clang! The sharp sound of metal against metal reverberated. Yuugo had blocked Kanon's sword just in time. "Oof!" As they pressed their swords together, Yuugo felt his feet sinking into the ground. He clenched his teeth as he stared at Kanon's confident smile. He was exhausted from the the battle he had already fought. If he lost focus for even one second, he knew he would be destroyed.

"Yuugo!" Tomoki planted his feet in the ground and pushed out his right fist. Green sparks flew from his clenched fist, and a flash of lightning spurted forth. Unfortunately, the beam of light suddenly changed direction right before it hit Kanon. "Shiki!"

Shiki had absorbed Tomoki's energy into his own fists. "Tomoki, I won't let you interfere with Master Kanon," he said carefully, clenching his raised fists.

Tomoki tried to support Yuugo many times, but Shiki blocked every one of his attempts. Even though they had the same powers, it was like a child fighting against an adult. But Tomoki wanted to do anything he could to help Yuugo. He mustered up all his strength and punched his fists out. Shiki sighed painfully and held his hand up over his head towards Tomoki. "Ahhhh!" Tomoki's face contorted with fear. A thin silver chain coiled around his wrists like a snake, up his wrist and then around his body. "Why, Shiki?" he cried angrily. Even as he looked at Shiki, who stood before him,

Tomoki could see that his brother did not look like a cruel person. "Why are you doing what that demon tells you to?" Tomoki looked up at his brother with frustrated tears in his eyes.

When he looked at Tomoki making a face like that, Shiki wanted to stretch out his arms to him. His indistinct memories suddenly came flooding back to him.

When his little brother would cry, Shiki would hurry to pick him up. "It's Onii-chan, Tomoki. It's okay." Whenever he would say that and smile, Tomoki would stop crying and look up at him innocently. Shiki would rub Tomoki's small, soft hand on his cheeks. His little brother was so cute; he adored him. His skin always smelled like milk.

"You've gotten so big, Tomoki," Shiki smiled nostalgically. Sometimes he would gaze at his family and his younger brother. He was filled with homesickness, but it had always seemed like he was seeing some kind of illusion. But he had watched over Tomoki as he had grown up. Strangely, he never harbored any jealousy or hatred towards his brother, who had grown up normally and happily. His world was Kanon, and he belonged to Kanon.

"Oniisan." When Tomoki called him that, his chest felt tight. Even though they hadn't seen each other for so long, they knew they were brothers. "Let's go home together! Mom and Dad never forgot about you, either!" he desperately pleaded with his brother, but Shiki shook his head quietly.

"I'm a demon. I can't live as a human anymore," Shiki whispered sadly. Behind them, a heroic struggle to the death between Kanon and Yuugo was unfolding.

The sounds of their swords striking against each other echoed in the darkness. Their swords shone, but moved so fast their eyes couldn't keep up with them. All they could see were the afterimages of their glittering blades. Yuugo lowered his sword and stared at Kanon with sharp eyes. Every muscle in his body reacted to his opponent's attacks. His instincts clung to survival. They were roughly equal in speed. But Yuugo was approaching his body's limit. When he had fought the giant monster Above Ground, he had taken a lot of damage. He couldn't let his guard down; he couldn't even blink. If he did, he knew Kanon would slaughter him.

His body reacted to Kanon's movement, and he thrust his katana upward. Kanon's golden hair fluttered in the air. "Damn you!" He narrowed his blue eyes with annoyance. Black blood ran down his cheek. His confident smile vanished, replaced with the brutal, bloodthirsty expression of a demon. Yuugo's katana sliced through the shoulder and front of Kanon's leather jacket. But that was when he reached his limit.

"Watch out!" He saw Tomoki scream at him in his peripheral vision. *Tomoki...* Suddenly, his consciousness faded. His opponent's blade drew near, and he covered himself with his left arm.

Crack! It was the sound of his bone breaking. Kanon's saber pierced through his arm guard and penetrated his skin. Yuugo mustered up all of his strength and somehow shook off Kanon's sword. He quickly jumped back, but his wings were already broken. He cringed in pain. The guard on his arm disappeared, and a large quantity of blood spurted from below his elbow. He clenched his teeth and took up his katana in his other hand.

Yuugo's broken arm hung loosely at his side, barely attached to his shoulder. Blood dripped down to his fingertips, and he felt himself growing faint. A burning pain raced through his body, like he was being burned alive. He felt like he was falling.

Kanon laughed cruelly and licked the blood off the blade of his saber. He narrowed his blue eyes. Suddenly, he thrust his saber deep into Yuugo's belly. "I love the look on your face." Kanon smiled with desire as he looked at his trophy. He twisted his sword, and its cold tip ripped right through Yuugo's wings and pushed out his back.

Even though the pain should have been unbearable, Yuugo didn't feel it. *Tomoki...* Through his slightly open eyelids, he saw Tomoki running over to him, his face wet with tears. *Run away...!!* Yuugo moved his lips, clutching the saber that stabbed through his stomach. Then, he coughed and blood spurted from his throat. He fell, still kneeling over, onto the hard ground.

"Nooooo! Yuugo!" Tomoki screamed. His eyes were wide open, wild with fear. His tears blurred his vision, and he shook his head. He had broken free from the chains that had bound his body.

"No, Tomoki!" Shiki pointed towards him, and Tomoki's body stiffened as if it had just received an electrical shock. The flash of light tied up Tomoki's body. The more he struggled to break free of the curse, the tighter his restraints became.

"No! Shiki...Oniisan! Stop it, stop it! Please save Yuugo!" Tomoki cried in a hoarse voice as he fell to the ground.

Kanon dragged Yuugo by his wings. "This is total darkness." He pointed to the huge hole that was in front of them. It was a crater several kilometers wide, and when he looked down into it, all he could see was an abyss of darkness. He tossed a rock into it, and it fell silently, not hitting anything on the way down. This meant there was probably no chance of being able to catch or hold onto anything if one fell down there.

It was as if time had stopped, but Yuugo's body automatically turned towards the depths of the darkness as if it was calling to him.

"Whether you're a demon or a human...if you fall in there, your existence becomes nothingness." Kanon gazed at the deep darkness. It was said that in the lowest layer of the earth, everything returned to nothingness. He did not know waited at the depths. No one had ever returned from them before. "This was fun," Kanon said with an amused look on his face.

The shoulder of his leather jacket had been ripped open, and his black demon blood flowed from his torn white skin. It mixed with Yuugo's blood, and Kanon's whole body was stained red and black.

Even if he tried to capture him, he knew Yuugo was

too strong. Kanon didn't show his pain on his face, but his heart was thumping inside. If Kanon hadn't struck first, he would have been the one who died. A cruel smile spread on his beautiful face. Even if demons' bodies were chopped up in this world, the pieces of them could gather together and be reborn. And those with souls and lives were even more troublesome; even if they lost their bodies, they could be reincarnated into a different one.

Kanon put a foot on Yuugo's back, grabbed a wing and tore it off. He cut it up so it couldn't come back, and then dropped it into the dark void. He would never let this man get in his way again...

"Stop it!" Tomoki screamed as loudly as he could. He was cursed by Shiki, but he tried to lift his heavy arms. As soon as he resisted, Tomoki's power would collide with Shiki's and intense green sparks would fly. The pain felt like he was being shot multiple times, and he clenched his teeth. He didn't have the energy to fight back against Shiki anymore. He bit his lip until he drew blood, and thrust his fists out towards Kanon. "Get away from Yuugo!" With all his might, he concentrated his energy and two spiral flashes of light exploded from his fingertips.

"Tomoki..." Shiki opened his eyes wide at the curse his brother had shot at Kanon, which wound around his body like a snake. But Tomoki was still under Shiki's curse. In order to stop Kanon from pushing Yuugo's body into the abyss, he had concentrated all of his strength towards him. But Tomoki's power still wasn't strong enough to completely seal Kanon.

"Shiki, take care of that brat!" Kanon cried angrily as he was bound by invisible chains. "It's an order. Kill him! And I'll bring you two together as one!"

"Yes..."

"Oniisan...Stop!" Tomoki pleaded desperately, as Shiki took a step forward. "Please...just save Yuugo," he begged. Since he was using all his energy to curse Kanon, Tomoki could not protect himself. "He's...really important to me," he said in a choked voice.

Shiki looked at Tomoki, who did not plead for his own life. He saw the reflection of his smiling face in his brother's tear-filled eyes. "Tomoki, take care of Mom and Dad," Shiki whispered gently as he touched his brother's cheek.

"What are you doing, Shiki?" Kanon roared like a beast as Shiki cursed him.

"Please forgive me, Master Kanon," Shiki whispered as he looked at Kanon with tears in his eyes. He stretched out his arms and hugged his master.

"Oniisan!" Tomoki screamed. Taking Kanon with him, Shiki's body disappeared into the crater.

Kanon struggled to break free of the curse.

As they fell into the dark void, Shiki whispered, "I'm sorry," as he stared into Kanon's blue eyes.

"You're my slave." Kanon roared as he held onto Shiki. "Don't ever disobey me!" His cruel voice was filled with hatred. Shiki's hands were bound behind him,

and he was pinned face-down on the bed. Shiki felt faint from the intense pain of Kanon's hard rod plunging into him. He screamed repeatedly.

Kanon ravaged Shiki's body like a starving beast. He pinned him down with his strong body, and pounded him over and over again.

This is how I'm going to die...Shiki thought as he pressed his face against the sheets. His trembling knees were spread apart, and Kanon grabbed his erection with his hands. His sharp nails dug into Shiki's head, and he wanted to scream. The room was filled with Shiki's cries and Kanon's rough, beast-like panting.

He slipped out of consciousness over and over again, but would wake up again from the pain, screaming. His nightmare wouldn't go away. Every time he opened his eyes, he found himself in the same room.

Shiki was remembering the first time Kanon raped him. He could not forget the pain and fear he felt that day. In that irrational and hopeless situation, Kanon was just a terrible, cruel demon. Shiki was so afraid he couldn't feel any hatred.

"Shiki..." He heard Kanon calling his name. *Shiki felt sharp teeth in his back and shoulders, and knew Kanon was sucking his blood. He was probably going to eat him because of his demon instincts. The bed sheets were stained with Shiki's blood. Even though Shiki was being raped, Kanon was yelling at him for losing consciousness. He was torturing Shiki in every way he knew how.*

The only reason Shiki could bear it was because he had heard Kanon speaking his true feelings once.

"You belong to me." Shiki was bleeding and close to death, and Kanon held his trembling hands. "You're my slave," he held Shiki's injured body like it was something precious. "Don't die..."

Shiki felt an unbearable sadness inside when he heard Kanon's voice. "Master Kanon..." I'll always be yours...

He felt Kanon's kisses on his cheek, and they were gentle—like a lover's. A tear rolled down Shiki's cheek.

"Shiki..."

Shiki slightly opened his eyes. Kanon's light blue eyes were staring only at him. His lips were slightly open. He looked like he was about to cry. Maybe that was the only human part of him that remained. Shana had created him for her amusement and called him a lump of mud. He had such a perfect, beautiful body, yet he despised anyone who was born with a "life" and "flesh." His intense yearning for those things had turned into hatred.

"Master Kanon..."

At that moment, Kanon stretched out his arms and buried his face in Shiki's chest. And, at that, Shiki had forgiven him. Just that once, he could not hate his cruel master. He was overwhelmed with affection for that sad demon.

The Underworld waited for them in the darkness where all bodies and souls became nothingness. It was very far from the real world Above Ground, where the sun shined. Tears poured from Shiki's eyes. "You never knew..." he whispered, as if confessing a sin he had hidden all his life. "I loved you..." He touched Kanon's lips with his own for the first time, weeping. "I'm so sorry, Master Kanon..."

"Who gave you permission...to do that..." Kanon said painfully to Shiki, who had collapsed in tears onto his chest. "You're my slave."

He held Shiki tightly in his arms. The curse had been broken. *My...Shiki...* Shiki felt Kanon's gentle voice reverberate in his chest, and, in their last moment, he answered in a tearful voice, "Yes, Master." In his arms, Shiki was finally able to smile happily...

"Oniisan!" Tomoki's tears continued to flow as he held the unconscious Yuugo against his chest. He had just felt his brother's consciousness flow into him. Waves of emotion flooded over him, and fragments of memories filled Tomoki, making him tremble. Shiki had told Kanon the feelings he had hidden for so long. Right before their deaths, their hearts had connected, and Shiki had been truly happy. His pain and sadness had been washed away, and he had been able to smile peacefully. That's how much he had loved that demon.

"Why?!" Tomoki cried for his brother, who had vanished. "He was such a cruel demon!" Kanon had tried to kill Yuugo, and had kept Shiki as a slave. He was responsible for an unfathomable massacre Above Ground; he was a demon that should be hated! "Why would you love someone like that?" He covered his face with both hands and cried. But no matter how angry he

was, he knew how his brother had felt. No matter how much Tomoki hated Kanon, he knew that Shiki loved him.

"Tomoki..." Yuugo slowly opened his eyes as he lay in Tomoki's lap.

"Yuugo!" Tomoki quickly grabbed Yuugo's outstretched hand.

"You got away safely...I'm so glad you're safe, Tomoki..." Yuugo whispered as he tried to endure the pain, on the verge of death. Tomoki held him in his arms and sobbed loudly, like a child.

It was the end of August, and they were in Yuugo's condo.

"I look pretty good in human form!" A black-haired man said as he admired himself in the bathroom mirror. When he smiled, small wrinkles formed around his eyes. He was very handsome. His age was uncertain; he could pass for twenty or even thirty. He was a bit shorter than Yuugo, but he was very muscular. "Lord Tomoki is going to fall for me!"

Tomoki was startled when someone called his name from the bathroom. "Is that you, Kurou?"

"Don't turn into a human!" Yuugo yelled and kicked Kurou violently from behind. Kurou transformed back into a crow and tumbled to the floor.

"Yuugo, you bastard! You are just afraid Lord Tomoki will fall in love with me!" Kurou righted himself and yelled at Yuugo, pointing one wing at him.

"Of course I'm not!"

"Yuugo!" Jade called in a cute voice as she came from the other room. She tugged on the hem of his shirt. "Buy me some pretty clothes!" She had beautiful blonde hair, white skin, and green eyes, but the little girl who appeared to be about six years old was wearing one of Yuugo's t-shirts. She still had cat ears, a tail, and even whiskers.

"Don't waste your energy transforming into a human, either!"

"Don't be rude to girls!" Jade said angrily, and her golden fur appeared again. Apparently, she really wanted to be a high school girl—but at this point, neither she nor Kurou were ready to appear in front of others. Since Tomoki the Barrier Master was nearby, they often came to visit Yuugo.

"I bought cake, want some?"

"Tomoki, don't spoil the monsters!"

"Yuugo, you're so narrow-minded!"

"Tomoki's nice, so even when I become a hot high school girl, I won't hit on Yuugo!"

"I don't want you to..." Yuugo replied. "Hurry up and go home to the Depths of Dreams."

"Now, now, Yuugo. Just think of us as pets. Just let us play a little!"

"I've never heard of such noisy pets!"

"I'm a little worried...Yuugo is getting meaner by the day!" Jade gave a motherly sigh as she licked the cake.

"It's your fault!"

"If you wanna be alone with Tomoki, why don't you just go into the bedroom?"

"Yeah, stay in there all night if you want. I want

to watch TV. I want to watch that sexy girl with the big boobs!" Kurou said. He clumsily opened the newspaper with a wing. "Television is amazing!"

"Mmm, this cake is good!"

After he locked the door, Yuugo brushed his hair out of his face. He was lucky they had brought the bed into the biggest room. Even though he wanted to be alone with Tomoki, every time he came over those monsters would always end up coming, too. And because they spent so much time watching television, they had even more to chatter noisily about.

"You can make them go back to the Depths of Dreams, right?"

"Yeah, but they're having so much fun. Let's just leave them alone." Tomoki smiled.

Yuugo sat down on the bed next to him, and his mood immediately improved when he saw Tomoki's smiling face. Even when the noisy monsters were around, Tomoki could forget about everything else.

"I'm so glad your wounds healed and you were able to come back here."

"Me, too." Yuugo put his arm around Tomoki's shoulders, and pressed his cheek against Tomoki's soft brown hair. Yuugo had just been able to come home the other day. He hadn't been able to move for about a month, and had recuperated in the Depths of Dreams. Tomoki had come to visit him every day, and he had heard the whole story about Kanon and Shiki from him.

Tomoki's sadness and pain didn't seem to be

easing. Yuugo was sure he would never forget it. When they heard about the victims of the massacre on the news, Tomoki was heartbroken about it. Yuugo told him, "You and Shiki were both victims of the demon, too." He didn't want Tomoki to feel responsible for anything that happened. "It's not our fault that we were born with these powers. Shiki wasn't the kind of person who got enjoyment from killing people, right?"

Tomoki had nodded his head in response. "It's not...Oniisan's fault!" He hadn't wanted to kill anyone. He was raised to obey Kanon's orders. Tomoki thought his brother had cursed the demon and jumped into the crater because he wanted to save Tomoki, his younger brother. And he wanted to end the pain of that demon, Kanon...

"Shiki protected this world," Yuugo had whispered as he combed his fingers through Tomoki's hair. He hadn't met Shiki, himself, but Yuugo knew he probably resembled Tomoki a lot, both in appearance and in spirit. And he had saved Yuugo's precious Tomoki...He wanted to sincerely thank Shiki for that.

"I'll always remember my brother..." Tomoki had whispered. White flower petals floated down from the pale pearl-colored sky above them. He didn't want to think that his brother had disappeared. "I hope he's in a place as peaceful as this ..."

"Me, too..." Yuugo answered as he gazed up at the sky. Tomoki was painfully beautiful as he cried silently. Yuugo wanted to hold him. At the same time, he wanted to be held by him.

"I love you, Yuugo." Tomoki whispered, burying

his face in Yuugo's chest. They only showed this kind of sweetness and affection to each other.

"I love you, too." Yuugo smiled gently. "I love you, Tomoki." He leaned over and gazed into Tomoki's eyes.

Even though Tomoki was used to it by now, that smile still made him blush. "I better not catch you smiling like that at anyone else!" He said firmly, his cheeks red. Yuugo tilted his head. "I'm really jealous and I want you all to myself, so you better be careful!" Tomoki continued and pointed a finger at him. Yuugo blinked his eyes in surprise.

"Ha ha ha...You're so cute, Tomoki," Yuugo whispered in Tomoki's ear and hugged him tightly to his chest.

"And you better not whisper like that to anyone else, either!"

"I won't."

"And you better not do this with anyone else, either..."

"I know."

Tomoki pushed his lover down on the bed and kissed him.

Afterword

Thank you for reading this book. This is the first time I've worked with Daria Novels. My name is Hikaru Yura, and I write boys' love, science fiction, occult, and fantasy stories. What did you think about Dark Walker? I'd be very happy to hear any comments.

This was a story about the world we go to when we fall asleep. The two main characters have the power to go to this world with their consciousness and mortal bodies still intact. This world originated from Hirotaka Kisaragi's manga series, which featured a brave girl as the protagonist. If you love science fiction and action, you should check out Kisaragi-sensei's comics.

I had just been thinking about writing an original story based on the setting of a manga when I was contacted by MOVIC-san about this project. Kisaragi-sensei's manga features completely different characters than this book. But they told me that he would do the illustrations for Dark Walker, so I immediately wanted to write about a character who had wings. (I'm actually a huge fan of black wings ... Kisaragi-sensei, I'm so sorry that I made you draw those complicated wings!) I tried my best to write both fight scenes and erotic scenes.

I'm so delighted at the beautiful illustrations. I was especially happy to see the cute scene between Shiki and Tomoki at the back of the book!

Thank you, Kisaragi-sensei!

In my case, if I don't think of the perfect names for my characters, I can't write my story. I decided on Kanon, Shiki, and Yuugo right away, but it took me a long time to come up with Tomoki's name. I tried writing numerous names next to Yuugo's, but he didn't like any of them except for Tomoki's! (laugh)

I found myself wanting to write more and more about the characters, including Kanon and Shiki. If I have the opportunity, I would love to write a sequel. I kept getting an extension on my deadline so I could write more and more, so I want to apologize to my editors and the publishing company! I'm sorry for the inconvenience. Thanks to everyone who helped me and who worked on this book.

-- Hikaru Yura

■ I DREW THIS PICTURE TO SHOW WHAT MIGHT HAVE HAPPENED HAD TOMOKI AND SHIKI GROWN UP TOGETHER NORMALLY. WHAT DO YOU THINK, YURA-SENSEI? I WAS DELIGHTED TO DO ILLUSTRATIONS FOR YURA-SENSEI'S NOVEL BASED ON MY MANGA. IT WAS ANOTHER SIDE OF THE "DEPTHS OF DREAMS," AND I CAN'T WAIT TO SEE WHAT KIND OF "DARK WALKERS" TOMOKI AND YUUGO TURN OUT TO BE.

■ AMONG THE CHARACTERS, KANON WAS THE EASIEST TO DRAW BUT HE WAS ALSO THE HARDEST FOR ME TO DECIDE HOW TO DRAW. I THINK HE MIGHT LOOK A LITTLE TOO MACHISMO—SORRY ABOUT THAT. I WAS REALLY FOND OF KANON AND SHIKI'S AWKWARD RELATIONSHIP. WELL, I HOPE WE'LL MEET AGAIN SOMETIME SOON...

-HIROTAKA KISARAGI

Love and Dysfunction
Under One Roof!!

CLEAR SKIES!

毎日晴天

Akira SUGANO &
Etsumi NINOMIYA

manga version

Clear Skies! Vol. 1   ISBN: 978-156970-575-9 $12.95
Clear Skies! Vol. 2   ISBN: 978-156970-576-6 $12.95

Volume 1 On Sale Now!

the original novel version

Clear Skies!
A Charming Love Story   ISBN: 978-156970-572-8 $8.95

June
junemanga.c

A CALL TO ARMS

A Novel
—— WRITTEN BY ——
TOW UBUKATA

蒼穹のファフナー

FAFNER
Dead Aggressor

Available Now!

ISBN:978-1-56970-820-0

$8.95

DMP
DIGITAL MANGA
PUBLISHING

GO DEEP UNDER COVER

written by
Saki Aida
英田サキ

illustrated by
Chiharu Nara
奈良千春

S エス

Volume 1
On Sale Now!

A NOVEL

Vol.1 ISBN:978-1-56970-706-7 $8.95
Vol.2 ISBN:978-1-56970-707-4 $8.95
Vol.3 ISBN:978-1-56970-708-1 $8.95
Vol.4 ISBN:978-1-56970-709-8 $8.95

TAIYOH
TOSHO

june

www.bs-garden.com

junemanga.com

Every Boss Needs A **HARD** worker

CAGED SLAVE
密室の虜

A Novel

Written by Yuiko Takamura

Illustrated by An Kanae

ISBN:#978-156970-735-7 $8.95

OAKLA PUBLISHING
www.oakla.com

june
junemanga.com

BRINGING NEW MEANING TO THE WORD

ANDROGYNY

A Novel
Written By: Kyoko Akitsu
Illustrated By: Tooko Miyagi
Creator of:
Il gatto sul G.

A Promise of Romance

契約――ブランドロマンス

Available Now!

ISBN: 978-156970-710-4

$8.95

Loyalty Paid In BLOOD

from

Satoru Ishihara

GOD of DOGS 犬の王

Available Now!

ISBN: 978-156970-587-2

$12.95

June™

junemanga.com

THE PULSING bite OF DEVOTION

MIKA SADAHIRO

PATHOS

Volume 1
On Sale Now!

Volume 1 ISBN:978-156970-560-5 $12.95
Volume 2 ISBN:978-156970-561-2 $12.95

OAKLA PUBLISHING
www.oakla.com

june
junemanga.com

A *Love* beyond *Time*

YUKARI HASHIDA

KABUKI

カブキ

Volume 1
On Sale Now!

Volume 1 ISBN:978-156970-592-6 $12.95
Volume 2 ISBN:978-156970-593-3 $12.95

june™

junemanga.com

he Only Exclusive Yaoi Store Online!
CLEAR SKIES!
VOL. 1
June
Forums
Contests
Prizes
And More!
Come join us!
Candy
LOG ON NOW!
www.yaoi-club.com

CONTINUES

Visit the website:
www.vampire-d.com

 DIGITAL MANGA PUBLISHING
www.dmpbooks.com